The Money Changers

UPTON SINCLAIR

DOVER PUBLICATIONS, INC.
Mineola, New York

Copyright

Note copyright © 2009 by Dover Publications, Inc.
All rights reserved.

Bibliographical Note

This Dover edition, first published in 2009, is an unabridged republication of the work first published by B. W. Dodge & Co., New York, in 1908. A new introductory note has been specially prepared for this edition.

Library of Congress Cataloging-in-Publication Data

Sinclair, Upton, 1878–1968.
    The money changers / Upton Sinclair.
        p. cm.
    Originally published: New York : B.W. Dodge & Co., 1908.
    ISBN-13: 978-0-486-46917-1
    ISBN-10: 0-486-46917-4
    1. Capitalists and financiers—Fiction. 2. Financial crises—Fiction. 3. New York (N.Y.)—Fiction. 4. Wall Street (New York, N.Y.)—Fiction. 5. Rich people—Fiction. 6. Speculation—Fiction. 7. Socialites—Fiction. I. Title.

PS3537.I85M5 2009
813'.52—dc22

                                                                2008038520

Manufactured in the United States of America
Dover Publications, Inc., 31 East 2nd Street, Mineola, N.Y. 11501

Note

AT AGE FOURTEEN Upton Sinclair (1878–1968) enrolled in City College of New York. He funded his college education by writing dime novels and stories for magazines and newspapers. It was at City College that Sinclair began to embrace socialist politics. In 1897 he enrolled in Columbia University for graduate work, determined to succeed academically while producing stories for various boys weeklies to pay for his continuing education.

After completing his graduate work at Columbia University, Sinclair was hired by a socialist journal, *Appeal to Reason*, to write about stockyard workers. It was through this journal that he spent several weeks researching and taking pictures for what became his best-known work, *The Jungle*. The work was serialized by *Appeal to Reason* in 1905, and then published by Doubleday in 1906. It was an immediate success selling more than 150,000 copies.

Sinclair's productivity and his ongoing and passionate interest in social and industrial reform underlie most of the ninety plus books he left us, including this topical and polemical novel—*The Money Changers*.

The Money Changers was first published in 1908. Sinclair wrote a historic novel concerning the real Wall Street Panic of 1907. In his fictionalized account, Sinclair describes how several formidable capitalists organize and orchestrate the fall of a rival trust company. The ruin of this trust company subsequently affects a stock market crash and a bank run by panicked citizens. The ultimate cost of this planned debacle is the loss of thousands of jobs, which throws the world into financial chaos.

One cannot help but draw parallels between what happens in

Upton Sinclair's fictionalized account with what has actually happened in the United States several times in recent decades. In the 1980s and 1990s, 747 Savings and Loans failed, which cost the government around $160 billion in bailouts. (In the end it will cost taxpayers $30 billion a year over thirty years.) The resulting taxpayer bailout ended up being even larger than it should have due to incentives built in for the directors of the Savings and Loans, which compounded the system's losses.

In March of 2008 Bear Stearns collapsed. In the six months that followed, Wall Street has seen its biggest restructuring since the Great Depression.

The federal government took control of Pasadena, California-based IndyMac Bank and its thirty-two branches in July 2008. After the takeover, the lines outside the bank went for blocks and fearful bank customers had to take numbers and wait (some for days) to withdraw funds—exactly what happened in Sinclair's fictional account of the failed bank trust.

In September 2008, the stock market plunged to a record one-day loss, all independent investment banks went out of business, and the world's largest insurance company—AIG—had to be taken over by the U.S. government. The two largest U.S. mortgage houses (Fannie Mae and Freddie Mac) were taken over, financial institutions went out of business, and some of the largest commercial banks were sold.

One-hundred years after *The Money Changers* was first published in 1908, the heads of some of these failed institutions have walked away with millions of dollars while citizens have lost their retirement savings.

What would Upton Sinclair have to say?

Rochelle Kronzek

CHAPTER I

"I am," said Reggie Mann, "quite beside myself to meet this Lucy Dupree."

"Who told you about her?" asked Allan Montague.

"Ollie's been telling everybody about her," said Reggie. "It sounds really wonderful. But I fear he must have exaggerated."

"People seem to develop a tendency to exaggeration," said Montague, "when they talk about Lucy."

"I am in quite a state about her," said Reggie.

Allan Montague looked at him and smiled. There were no visible signs of agitation about Reggie. He had come to take Alice to church, and he was exquisitely groomed and perfumed, and wore a wonderful scarlet orchid in his buttonhole. Montague, lounging back in a big leather chair and watching him, smiled to himself at the thought that Reggie regarded Lucy as a new kind of flower, with which he might parade down the Avenue and attract attention.

"Is she large or small?" asked Reggie.

"She is about your size," said Montague—which was very small indeed.

Alice entered at this moment in a new spring costume. Reggie sprang to his feet, and greeted her with his inevitable effusiveness.

Then he asked, "Do you know her, too?"

"Who? Lucy?" asked Alice. "I went to school with her."

"Judge Dupree's plantation was next to ours," said Montague. "We all grew up together."

"There was hardly a day that I did not see her until she was

1

married," said Alice. "She was married at seventeen, you know—to a man much older than herself."

"We have never seen her since that," added the other. "She has lived in New Orleans."

"And only twenty-two now," exclaimed Reggie. "All the wisdom of a widow and the graces of an *ingénue!*" And he raised his hands with a gesture of admiration.

"Has she got money?" he asked.

"She had enough for New Orleans," was the reply. "I don't know about New York."

"Ah well," he said meditatively, "there's plenty of money lying about."

He took Alice away to her devotions, leaving Montague to the memories which the mention of Lucy Dupree awakened.

Allan Montague had been in love with Lucy half a dozen times in his life; it had begun when she was a babe in arms, and continued intermittently until her marriage. Lucy was a beauty of the creole type, with raven-black hair and gorgeous colouring; and Allan carried with him everywhere the face of joy, with the quick, mobile features across which tears and laughter chased like April shower across the sky.

Lucy was a tiny creature, as he had said, but she was a well-spring of abounding energy. She had been the life of a lonely household from the first hour, and all who came near her yielded to her spell. Allan remembered one occasion when he had entered the house and seen the grave and venerable chief justice of the State down upon his hands and knees, with Lucy on his back.

She was a born actress, everybody said. When she was no more than four, she would lie in bed when she should have been asleep, and tell herself tragic stories to make her weep. Before long she had discovered several chests full of the clothes which her mother had worn in the days when she was a belle of the old plantation society; and then Lucy would have tableaus and theatricals, and would astonish all beholders in the rôle of an Oriental princess or a Queen of the Night.

Her mother had died when she was very young, and she had grown up with only her father for a companion. Judge Dupree was one of the rich men of the neighbourhood, and he lavished everything upon his daughter; but people had said that Lucy would suffer for the lack of a woman's care, and the prophecy had been tragically fulfilled. There had come a man, much older than herself, but with a glamour of romance about him; and the wonder of love had suddenly revealed itself to Lucy, and swept her away as no emotion had ever done before.

One day she disappeared, and Montague had never seen her again. He knew that she had gone to New Orleans to live, and he heard rumours that she was very unhappy, that her husband was a spendthrift and a rake. Scarcely a year after her marriage Montague heard the story of his death by an accident while driving.

He had heard no more until a short time after his coming to New York, when the home papers had reported the death of Judge Dupree. And then a week or so ago had come a letter from Lucy, to his brother, Oliver Montague, saying that she was coming to New York, perhaps to live permanently, and asking him to meet her and to engage accommodation for her in some hotel.

Montague wondered what she would be like when he saw her again. He wondered what five years of suffering and experience would have done for her; whether it would have weakened her enthusiasm and dried up her springs of joy. Lucy grown serious was something that was difficult for him to imagine.

And then again would come a mood of doubt, when he distrusted the thrill which the memory of her brought. Would she be able to maintain her spell in competition with what life had brought him since?

His reverie was broken by Oliver, who came in to ask him if he wished to go to meet her. "Those Southern trains are always several hours late," he said. "I told my man to go over and 'phone me."

"You are to have her in charge," said Montague; "you had better see her first. Tell her I will come in the evening." And so he went to the great apartment hotel—the same to which Oliver had originally introduced him. And there was Lucy.

She was just the same. He could see it in an instant; there was the same joyfulness, the same eagerness; there was the same beauty, which had made men's hearts leap up. There was not a line of care upon her features—she was like a perfect flower come to its fulness.

She came to him with both her hands outstretched. "Allan!" she cried, "Allan! I am so glad to see you!" And she caught his hands in hers and stood and gazed at him. "My, how big you have grown, and how serious! Isn't he splendid, Ollie?"

Oliver stood by, watching. He smiled dryly. "He is a trifle too epic for me," he said.

"Oh, my, how wonderful it seems to see you!" she exclaimed. "It makes me think of fifty things at once. We must sit down and have a long talk. It will take me all night to ask you all the questions I have to."

Lucy was in mourning for her father, but she had contrived to make her costume serve as a frame for her beauty. She seemed like a flaming ruby against a background of black velvet. "Tell me how you have been?" she rushed on. "And what has happened to you up here? How is your mother?"

"Just the same," said Montague; "she wants you to come round to-morrow morning."

"I will," said Lucy—"the first thing, before I go anywhere. And Mammy Lucy! How is Mammy Lucy?"

"She is well," he replied. "She's beside herself to see you."

"Tell her I am coming," said she. "I would rather see Mammy Lucy than the Brooklyn Bridge!"

She led him to a seat, placed herself opposite him, devouring him with her eyes. "It makes me seem like a girl again to see you," she said.

"Do you count yourself aged?" asked Montague, laughing.

"Oh, I feel old," said Lucy, with a sudden look of fear—"you have no idea, Allan. But I don't want anybody to know about it!" And then she cried eagerly, "Do you remember the swing in the orchard? And do you remember the pool where the big alligator lived? And the persimmons? And Old Joe?"

Allan Montague remembered all these things; in the course of the half-hour that followed he remembered pretty nearly all the exciting adventures which he and Oliver and Lucy had had since Lucy was old enough to walk. And he told her the latest news about all their neighbours, and about all the servants whom she remembered. He told her also about his father's death, and how the house had been burned, and how they had sold the plantation and come North.

"And how are you doing, Allan?" she asked.

"I am practising law," he said. "I'm not making a fortune, but I'm managing to pay my bills. That is more than some other people do in this city."

"I should imagine it," said Lucy. "With all that row of shops on Fifth Avenue! Oh, I know I shall spend all that I own in the first week. And this hotel—why, it's perfectly frightful."

"Oliver has told you the prices, has he?" said Montague, with a laugh.

"He has taken my breath away," said Lucy. "How am I ever to manage such things?"

"You will have to settle that with him," said Montague. "He has taken charge, and he doesn't want me to interfere."

"But I want your advice," said Lucy. "You are a business man, and Ollie never was anything but a boy."

"Ollie has learned a good deal since he has been in New York," the other responded.

"I can tell you my side of the case very quickly," he went on, after a moment's pause. "He brought me here, and persuaded me that this was how I ought to live if I wanted to get into Society. I tried it for a while, but I found that I did not like the things I had to do, and so I quit. You will find us in an apartment a couple of blocks farther from Fifth Avenue, and we only pay about one-tenth as much for it. And now, whether you follow me or Ollie depends upon whether you want to get into Society."

Lucy wrinkled her brows in thought. "I didn't come to New York to bury myself in a boarding-house," she said. "I *do* want to meet people."

"Well," said Montague, "Oliver knows a lot of them, and he will introduce you. Perhaps you will like them—I don't know. I am sure you won't have any difficulty in making them like you."

"Thank you, sir," said Lucy. "You are as ingenuous as ever!"

"I don't want to say anything to spoil your pleasure," said the other. "You will find out about matters for yourself. But I feel like telling you this—don't *you* be too ingenuous. You can't trust people quite so freely here as you did at home."

"Thank you," said Lucy. "Ollie has already been lecturing me. I had no idea it was such a serious matter to come to New York. I told him that widows were commonly supposed to know how to take care of themselves."

"I had a rather bad time of it myself, getting adjusted to things," said Montague, smiling. "So you must make allowances for my forebodings."

"I've told Lucy a little about it," put in Oliver dryly.

"He told me a most fascinating love-story!" said Lucy, gazing at him with a mischievous twinkle in her eyes. "I shall certainly look out for the dazzling Mrs. Winnie."

"You may meet her to-morrow night," put in Oliver. "You are invited to dinner at Mrs. Billy Alden's."

"I have read about Mrs. Billy in the newspapers," said Lucy. "But I never expected to meet her. How in the world has Oliver managed to jump so into the midst of things?"

Oliver undertook to explain; and Montague sat by, smiling to himself over his brother's carefully expurgated account of his own social career. Oliver had evidently laid his plans to take charge of Lucy, and to escort her to a high seat upon the platform of Society.

"But tell me, all this will cost so much money!" Lucy protested. "And I don't want to have to marry one of these terrible millionaires."

She turned to Montague abruptly. "Have you got an office somewhere down town?" she asked. "And may I come to-morrow, and see you, and get you to be my business adviser? Old Mr. Holmes is dead, you know. He used to be father's lawyer, and he knew all about my affairs. He never thought it worth while to explain anything to me, so now I don't know very well what I have or what I can do."

"I will do all I can to help you," Montague answered.

"And you must be very severe with me," Lucy continued,

"and not let me spend too much money, or make any blunders. That was the way Mr. Holmes used to do, and since he is dead, I have positively been afraid to trust myself about."

"If I am to play that part for you," said Montague, laughing, "I am afraid we'll very soon clash with my brother."

Montague had very little confidence in his ability to fill the part. As he watched Lucy, he had a sense of tragedy impending. He knew enough to feel sure that Lucy was not rich, according to New York standards of wealth; and he felt that the lure of the city was already upon her. She was dazzled by the vision of automobiles and shops and hotels and theatres, and all the wonders which these held out to her. She had come with all her generous enthusiasms; and she was hungry with a terrible hunger for life.

Montague had been through the mill, and he saw ahead so clearly that it was impossible for him not to try to guide her, and to save her from the worst of her mistakes. Hence arose a strange relationship between them; from the beginning Lucy made him her confidant, and told him all her troubles. To be sure, she never took his advice; she would say, with her pretty laugh, that she did not want him to keep her out of trouble, but only to sympathize with her afterwards. And Montague followed her; he told himself again and again that there was no excuse for Lucy; but all the while he was making excuses.

She went over the next morning to see Oliver's mother, and Mammy Lucy, who had been named after her grandmother. Then in the afternoon she went shopping with Alice—declaring that it was impossible for her to appear anywhere in New York until she had made herself "respectable." And then in the evening Montague called for her, and took her to Mrs. Billy Alden's Fifth Avenue palace.

On the way he beguiled the time by telling her about the terrible Mrs. Billy and her terrible tongue; and about the war between the great lady and her relatives, the Wallings. "You must not be surprised," he said, "if she pins you in a corner and asks all about you. Mrs. Billy is a privileged character, and the conventions do not apply to her."

Montague had come to take the Alden magnificence as a matter of course by this time, but he felt Lucy thrill with excitement at the vision of the Doge's palace, with its black marble carvings and its lackeys in scarlet and gold. Then came Mrs. Billy herself, resplendent in dark purple brocade, with a few ropes of pearls flung about her neck. She was almost tall enough to look over the top of Lucy's head, and she stood away a little, so as to look at her comfortably.

"I tried to have Mrs. Winnie here for you," she said to Montague, as she placed him at her right hand. "But she was not able to come, so you will have to make out with me."

"Have you many more beauties like that down in Mississippi?" she asked, when they were seated. "If so, I don't see why you came up here."

"You like her, do you?" he asked.

"I like her looks," said Mrs. Billy. "Has she got any sense? It is quite impossible to believe that she's a widow. She needs someone to take care of her just the same."

"I will recommend her to your favour," said Montague. "I have been telling her about you."

"What have you told her?" asked Mrs. Billy serenely—"that I win too much money at bridge, and drink Scotch at dinner?" Then, seeing Montague blush furiously, she laughed. "I know it is true. I have caught you thinking it half a dozen times."

And she reached out for the decanter which the butler had just placed in front of her, and proceeded to help herself to her opening glass.

Montague told her all about Lucy; and, in the meantime, he watched the latter, who sat near the centre of the table, talking with Stanley Ryder. Montague had played bridge with this man once or twice at Mrs. Winnie's, and he thought to himself that Lucy could hardly have met a man who would embody in himself more of the fascinations of the Metropolis. Ryder was president of the Gotham Trust Company, an institution whose magnificent marble front was one of the sights of Fifth Avenue. He was a man a trifle under fifty, tall and distinguished-looking, with an iron-grey moustache, and the manners of a diplomat. He was not only a banker, he was also a man of culture; he had

run away to sea in his youth, and he had travelled in every country of the world. He was also a bit of an author, in an amateur
way, and if there was any book which he had not dipped into, it
was not a book of which one would be apt to hear in Society. He
could talk upon any subject, and a hostess who could secure
Stanley Ryder for one of her dinner-parties generally counted
upon a success. "He doesn't go out much, these busy days," said
Mrs. Billy. "But I told him about your friend."

Now and then the conversation at the table would become
general, and Montague noticed that it was always Ryder who
led. His flashes of wit shot back and forth across the table; and
those who matched themselves against him seldom failed to
come off the worse. It was an unscrupulous kind of wit, dazzling
and dangerous. Ryder was the type of man one met now and
then in Society, who had adopted radical ideas for the sake of
being distinguished. It was a fine thing for a man who had made
a brilliant success in a certain social environment to shatter in
his conversation all the ideals and conventions of that environment, and thus to reveal how little he really cared for the success which he had won.

It was very entertaining at a dinner-party; but Montague
thought to himself with a smile how far was Stanley Ryder from
the type of person one imagined as the head of an enormous and
flourishing bank. When they had adjourned to the drawing-
room, he capped the climax of the incongruity by going to the
piano and playing a movement from some terrible Russian
suite.

Afterwards Montague saw him stroll off to the conservatory
with Lucy Dupree. There were two people too many for bridge,
and that was a good excuse; but none the less Montague felt
restless during the hours that he sat at table and let Mrs. Billy
win his money.

After the ordeal was over and the party had broken up, he
found his friend sitting by the side of the fountain in Mrs. Billy's
conservatory, gazing fixedly in front of her, while Ryder at her
side was talking.

"You met an interesting man," he said, when they had got
settled in the carriage.

"One of the most extraordinary men I ever met," said Lucy, quickly. "I wish that you would tell me about him. Do you know him well?"

"I have heard him talk some, and I know him in a business way."

"Is he so very rich?" she asked.

"He has a few millions," said he. "And I suppose he is turning them over very rapidly. People say that he is a daring speculator."

"A speculator!" exclaimed Lucy. "Why, I thought that he was the president of a bank!"

"When you have been in New York a while," said Montague, with a smile, "you will realize that there is nothing incompatible in the two."

Lucy was silent, a little staggered at the remark. "I am told," Montague added, with a smile, "that even Ryder's wife won't keep her money in the Gotham Trust."

Montague had not anticipated the effect of this remark. Lucy gave a sudden start. "His wife!" she exclaimed.

"Why, yes," said Montague. "Didn't you know that he was married?"

"No," said Lucy, in a low voice; "I did not."

There was a long silence. Finally she asked, "Why was not his wife invited to the dinner?"

"They seldom go out together," said Montague.

"Have they separated?" she asked.

"There is a new and fashionable kind of separation," was the answer. "They live in opposite sides of a large mansion, and meet on formal occasions."

"What sort of a woman is she?" asked Lucy.

"I don't know anything about her," he replied.

There was a silence again. Finally Montague said, "There is no cause to be sorry for him, you understand."

And Lucy touched his hand lightly with hers.

"That's all right, Allan," she said. "Don't worry. I am not apt to make the same mistake twice."

It seemed to Montague that there was nothing to be said after that.

CHAPTER II

Lucy wanted to come down to Montague's office to talk business with him; but he would not put her to that trouble, and called the next morning at her apartment before he went down town. She showed him all her papers; her father's will, with a list of his property, and also the accounts of Mr. Holmes, and the rent-roll of her properties in New Orleans. As Montague had anticipated, Lucy's affairs had not been well managed, and he had many matters to look into and many questions to ask. There were a number of mortgages on real estate and buildings, and, on the other hand, some of Lucy's own properties were mortgaged, a state of affairs which she was not able to explain. There were stocks in several industrial companies, of which Montague knew but little. Last, and most important of all, there was a block of five thousand shares in the Northern Mississippi Railroad.

"You know all about that, at any rate," said Lucy. "Have you sold your own holdings yet?"

"No," said Montague. "Father wished me to keep the agreement as long as the others did."

"I am free to sell mine, am I not?" asked Lucy.

"I should certainly advise you to sell it," said Montague. "But I am afraid it will not be easy to find a purchaser."

The Northern Mississippi was a railroad with which Montague had grown up, so to speak; there was never a time in his recollection when the two families had not talked about it. It ran from Atkin to Opala, a distance of about fifty miles, connecting at the latter point with one of the main lines of the State. It was an enterprise which Judge Dupree had planned, as a means of

opening up a section of country in the future of which he had
faith.

It had been undertaken at a time when distrust of Wall Street
was very keen in that neighbourhood; and Judge Dupree had
raised a couple of million dollars among his own friends and
neighbours, adding another half-million of his own, with a gentleman's agreement among all of them that the road would not
ask favours of Northern capitalists, and that its stock should
never be listed on the Exchanges. The first president had been
an uncle of Lucy's, and the present holder of the office was an
old friend of the family's.

But the sectional pride which had raised the capital could not
furnish the traffic. The towns which Judge Dupree had imagined did not materialize, and the little railroad did not keep pace
with the progress of the time. For the last decade or so its properties had been depreciating and its earnings falling off, and it
had been several years since Montague had drawn any dividends upon the fifty thousand dollars' worth of stock for which
his father had paid par value.

He was reminded, as he talked about all this with Lucy, of a
project which had been mooted some ten or twelve years ago,
to extend the line from Atkin so as to connect with the plant of
the Mississippi Steel Company, and give that concern a direct
outlet toward the west. The Mississippi Steel Company had one
of the half dozen largest plate and rail mills in the country, and
the idea of directing even a small portion of its enormous freight
was one which had incessantly tantalized the minds of the directors of the Northern Mississippi.

They had gone so far as to conduct a survey, and to make a
careful estimate of the cost of the proposed extension. Montague
knew about this, because it had chanced that he, together with
Lucy's brother, who was now in California, had spent part of his
vacation on a hunting trip, during which they had camped near
the surveying party. The proposed line had to find its way
through the Talula swamps, and here was where the uncertainty
of the project came in. There were a dozen routes proposed,
and Montague remembered how he had sat by the camp-fire
one evening, and got into conversation with one of the younger

men of the party, and listened to his grumbling about the blun-
dering of the survey. It was his opinion that the head-surveyor
was incompetent, that he was obstinately rejecting the best
routes in favour of others which were almost impossible.

Montague had taken this gossip to his father, but he did not
know whether his father had ever looked into the matter. He
only knew that when the project for the proposed extension had
been brought up at a stockholders' meeting, the cost of the work
was found so great that it was impossible to raise the money. A
proposal to go to the Mississippi Steel Company was voted
down, because Mississippi Steel was in the hands of Wall Street
men; and neither Judge Dupree nor General Montague had
realized at that time the hopelessness of the plight of the little
railroad.

All these matters were brought up in the conversation
between Lucy and Montague. There was no reason, he assured
her, why they should still hold on to their stock; if, by the proposed extension, or by any other plan, new capitalists could
make a success of the company, it would be well to make some
combination with them, or, better yet, to sell out entirely.
Montague promised that he would take the matter in hand and
see what he could do.

His first thought, as he went down town, was of Jim Hegan.
"Come and see me sometime," Hegan had said, and Montague
had never accepted the invitation. The Northern Mississippi
would, of course, be a mere bagatelle to a man like Hegan, but
who could tell what new plans he might be able to fit it into?
Montague knew by the rumours in the street that the great
financier had sold out all his holdings in two or three of his most
important ventures.

He went at once to Hegan's office, in the building of one of
the great insurance companies down town. He made his way
through corridors of marble to a gate of massively ornamented
bronze, behind which stood a huge guardian in uniform, also
massively ornamented. Montague generally passed for a big
man, but this personage made him feel like an office-boy.

"Is Mr. Hegan in?" he asked.

"Do you call by appointment?" was the response.

"Not precisely," said Montague, producing a card. "Will you kindly send this to Mr. Hegan?"

"Do you know Mr. Hegan personally?" the man demanded.

"I do," Montague answered.

The other had made no sign, as far as Montague could make out, but at this moment a dapper young secretary made his appearance from the doors behind the gate. "Would you kindly state the business upon which you wish to see Mr. Hegan?" he said.

"I wish to see Mr. Hegan personally," Montague answered, with just a trifle of asperity. "If you will kindly take in this card, it will be sufficient."

He submitted with what grace he could to a swift inspection at the secretary's hands, wondering, in the meantime, if his new spring overcoat was sufficiently up-to-date to entitle him, in the secretary's judgment, to be a friend of the great man within. Finally the man disappeared with the card, and half a minute later came back, smiling effusively. He ushered Montague into a huge office with leather-cushioned chairs large enough to hold several people each, and too large for any one person to be comfortable in. There was a map of the continent upon the wall, across which Jim Hegan's railroads stretched like scarlet ribbons. There were also heads of bison and reindeer, which Hegan had shot himself.

Montague had to wait only a minute or two, and then he was escorted through a chain of rooms, and came at last to the magnate's inner sanctum. This was plain, with an elaborate and studied plainness, and Jim Hegan sat in front of a flat mahogany desk which had not a scrap of paper anywhere upon it.

He rose as the other came in, stretching out his huge form. "How do you do, Mr. Montague?" he said, and shook hands. Then he sat down in his chair, and settled back until his head rested on the back, and bent his great beetling brows, and gazed at his visitor.

The last time that Montague had met Hegan they had talked about horses, and about old days in Texas; but Montague was wise enough to realize that this had been in the evening. "I have come on a matter of business, Mr. Hegan," he said. "So I will be as brief as possible."

"A course of action which I do my best to pardon," was the smiling reply.

"I want to propose to you to interest yourself in the affairs of the Northern Mississippi Railroad," said the other.

"The Northern Mississippi?" said Hegan, knitting his brows. "I have never heard of it."

"I don't imagine that many people have," the other answered, and went on to tell the story of the line.

"I have five hundred shares of the stock myself," he said, "but it has been in my family for a long time, and I am perfectly satisfied to let it stay there. I am not making this proposition on my own account, but for a client who has a block of five thousand shares. I have here the annual reports of the road for several years, and some other information about its condition. My idea was that you might care to take the road, and make the proposed extension to the works of the Mississippi Steel Company."

"Mississippi Steel!" exclaimed Hegan. He had evidently heard of that.

"How long ago did you say it was that this plan was looked into?" he asked. And Montague told him the story of the survey, and what he himself had heard about it.

"That sounds curious," said Hegan, and bent his brows, evidently in deep thought. "I will look into the matter," he said finally. "I have no plans of my own that would take me into that neighbourhood, but it may be possible that I can think of someone who would be interested. Have you any idea what your client wants for the thousand shares?"

"My client has put the matter into my hands," he answered. "The matter was only broached to me this morning, and I shall have to look further into the condition of the road. I should advise her to accept a fair offer—say seventy-five per cent of the par value of the stock."

"We can talk about that later," said Hegan, "if I can find the man for you." And Montague shook hands with him and left.

He stepped in on his way home in the evening to tell Lucy

about the result of his interview. "We shall hear from him soon," he said. "I don't imagine that Hegan is a man who takes long to make up his mind."

"My prayers will be with him," said Lucy, with a laugh. Then she added, "I suppose I shall see you Friday night at Mr. Harvey's."

"I shan't come out until Saturday afternoon," said he. "I am very busy these days, working on a case. But I try to find time to get down to Siegfried Harvey's; I seem to get along with him."

"They tell me he goes in for horses," said Lucy.

"He has a splendid stable," he answered.

"It was good of Ollie to bring him round," said she. "I have certainly jumped into the midst of things. What do you think I'm going to do to-morrow?"

"I have no idea," he said.

"I have been invited to see Mr. Waterman's art gallery."

"Dan Waterman's!" he exclaimed. "How did that happen?"

"Mrs. Alden's brother asked me. He knows him, and got me the invitation. Wouldn't you like to go?"

"I shall be busy in court all day to-morrow," said Montague. "But I'd like to see the collection. I understand it's a wonderful affair—the old man has spent all his spare time at it. You hear fabulous estimates of what it's cost him—four or five millions at the least."

"But why in the world does he hide it in a studio way up the Hudson?" cried Lucy.

The other shrugged his shoulders. "Just a whim," he said. "He didn't collect it for other people's pleasure."

"Well, so long as he lets me see it, I can't complain," said Lucy. "There are so many things to see in this city, I am sure I shall be busy for a year."

"You will get tired before you have seen half of them," he answered. "Everybody does."

"Do you know Mr. Waterman?" she asked.

"I have never met him," he said. "I have seen him a couple of times." And Montague went on to tell her of the occasion in the Millonaires' Club, when he had seen the Crœsus of Wall Street surrounded by an attending throng of "little millionaires."

"I hope I shan't meet him," said Lucy. "I know I should be frightened to death."

"They say he can be charming when he wants to," replied Montague. "The ladies are fond of him."

On Saturday afternoon, when Montague went down to Harvey's Long Island home, his brother met him at the ferry.

"Allan," he began immediately, "did you know that Lucy had come down here with Stanley Ryder?"

"Heavens, no!" exclaimed Montague. "Is Ryder down here?"

"He got Harvey to invite him," Oliver replied. "And I know it was for no reason in the world but to be with Lucy. He took her out in his automobile."

Montague was dumfounded.

"She never hinted it to me," he said.

"By God!" exclaimed Oliver, "I wonder if that fellow is going after Lucy!"

Montague stood for some time lost in sombre thought. "I don't think it will do him much good," he said. "Lucy knows too much."

"Lucy has never met a man like Stanley Ryder!" declared the other. "He has spent all his life hunting women, and she is no match for him at all."

"What do you know about him?" asked Montague.

"What don't I know about him!" exclaimed the other. "He was in love with Betty Wyman once."

"Oh, my Lord!" exclaimed Montague.

"Yes," said Oliver, "and she told me all about it. He has as many tricks as a conjurer. He has read a lot of New Thought stuff, and he talks about his yearning soul, and every woman he meets is his affinity. And then again, he is a free-thinker, and he discourses about liberty and the rights of women. He takes all the moralities and shuffles them up, until you'd think the noblest rôle a woman could play is that of a married man's mistress."

Montague could not forbear to smile. "I have known you to shuffle the moralities now and then yourself, Ollie," he said.

"Yes, that's all right," replied the other. "But this is Lucy. And somebody's got to talk to her about Stanley Ryder."

"I will do it," Montague answered.

He found Lucy in a cosy corner of the library when he came down to dinner. She was full of all the wonderful things that she had seen in Dan Waterman's art gallery. "And, Allan," she exclaimed, "what do you think, I met him!"

"You don't mean it!" said he.

"He was there the whole afternoon!" declared Lucy. "And he never did a thing but be nice to me!"

"Then you didn't find him so terrible as you expected," said Montague.

"He was perfectly charming," said Lucy. "He showed me his whole collection and told me the history of the different paintings, and stories about how he got them. I never had such an experience in my life."

"He can be an interesting man when he chooses," Montague responded.

"He is marvellous!" said she. "You look at that lean figure, and the wizened-up old hawk's face, with the white hair all round it, and you'd think that he was in his dotage. But when he talks—I don't wonder men obey him!"

"They obey him!" said Montague. "No mistake about that! There is not a man in Wall Street who could live for twenty-four hours if old Dan Waterman went after him in earnest."

"How in the world does he do it?" asked Lucy. "Is he so enormously rich?"

"It is not the money he owns," said Montague; "it's what he controls. He is master of the banks; and no man can take a step in Wall Street without his knowing it if he wants to. And he can break a man's credit; he can have all his loans called. He can swing the market so as to break a man. And then, think of his power in Washington! He uses the Treasury as if it were one of his branch offices."

"It seems frightful," said Lucy. "And that old man—over eighty! I'm glad that I met him, at any rate."

She paused, seeing Stanley Ryder in the doorway. He was evidently looking for her. He took her in to dinner; and every now and then, when Montague stole a glance at her, he saw that Ryder was monopolizing her attention.

After dinner they adjourned to the music-room, and Ryder played a couple of Chopin's Nocturnes. He never took his eyes from Lucy's face while he was playing. "I declare," remarked Betty Wyman in Montague's hearing, "the way Stanley Ryder makes love at the piano is positively indecent."

Montague dodged several invitations to play cards, and deliberately placed himself at Lucy's side for the evening. And when at last Stanley Ryder had gone away in disgust to the smoking-room, he turned to her and said, "Lucy, you must let me speak to you about this."

"I don't mind your speaking to me, Allan," she said, with a feeble attempt at a smile.

"But you must pay attention to me," he protested. "You really don't know the sort of man you are dealing with, or what people think about him."

She sat in silence, biting her lip nervously, while Montague told her, as plainly as he could, what Ryder's reputation was. All that she could answer was, "He is such an interesting man!"

"There are many interesting men," said he, "but you will never meet them if you get people talking about you like this."

Lucy clasped her hands together.

"Allan," she exclaimed, "I did my best to persuade him not to come out here. And you are right. I will do what you say—I will have nothing to do with him, honestly. You shall see! It's his own fault that he came, and he can find somebody else to entertain him while he's here."

"I wish that you would tell him plainly, Lucy," said Montague. "Never mind if he gets angry. Make him understand you—once for all."

"I will—I will!" she declared.

And Montague judged that she carried out her promise quickly, for the rest of the evening Ryder gave to entertaining the company. About midnight Montague chanced to look into the library, and he saw the president of the Gotham Trust in the midst of a group which was excitedly discussing divorce. "Marriage is a sin for which the Church refuses absolution!" he heard Stanley Ryder exclaiming.

CHAPTER III

A few days after these incidents, Montague was waiting for a friend who was to come to dinner at his hotel. He was sitting in the lobby reading a paper, and he noticed an elderly gentleman with a grey goatee and rather florid complexion who passed down the corridor before him. A minute or two later he happened to glance up, and he caught this gentleman's eye.

The latter started, and a look of amazement came over his face. He came forward, saying, "I beg pardon, but is not this Allan Montague?"

"It is," said Montague, looking at him in perplexity.

"You don't remember me, do you?" said the other.

"I must confess that I do not," was the answer.

"I am Colonel Cole."

But Montague only knitted his brows in greater perplexity. "Colonel Cole?" he repeated.

"You were too young to remember me," the other said. "I have been at your house a dozen times. I was in your father's brigade."

"Indeed!" exclaimed Montague. "I beg your pardon."

"Don't mention it, don't mention it," said the other, taking a seat beside him. "It was really extraordinary that I should recall you. And how is your brother? Is he in New York?"

"He is," said Montague.

"And your mother? She is still living, I trust?"

"Oh yes," said he. "She is in this hotel."

"It is really an extraordinary pleasure!" exclaimed the other. "I did not think I knew a soul in New York."

"You are visiting here?" asked Montague.

"From the West," said the Colonel.

"It is curious how things follow out," he continued, after a pause. "I was thinking about your father only this very day. I had a proposal from someone who wanted to buy some stock that I have—in the Northern Mississippi Railroad."

Montague gave a start. "You don't mean it!" he said.

"Yes," said the other. "Your father persuaded me to take some of the stock, away back in the old days. And I have had it ever since. I had forgotten all about it."

Montague smiled. "When you have disposed of yours," he said, "you might refer your party to me. I know of some more that is for sale."

"I have no doubt," said the Colonel. "But I fancy it won't fetch much now. I don't remember receiving any dividends."

There was a pause. "It is a curious coincidence," said the other. "I, too, have been thinking about the railroad. My friend, Mrs. Taylor, has just come up from New Orleans. She used to be Lucy Dupree."

The Colonel strove to recall. "Dupree?" he said.

"Judge Dupree's daughter," said Montague. "His brother, John Dupree, was the first president of the road."

"Oh yes," said the Colonel. "Of course, of course! I remember the Judge now. Your father told me he had taken quite a lot of the stock."

"Yes, he was the prime mover in the enterprise."

"And who was that other gentleman?" said the Colonel, racking his brains. "The one who used to be so much in his house, and was so much interested in him——"

"You mean Mr. Lee Gordon?" said Montague.

"Yes, I think that was the name," the other replied.

"He was my father's cousin," said Montague. "He put so much money into the road that the family has been poor ever since."

"It was an unfortunate venture," said the Colonel. "It is too bad some of our big capitalists don't take it up and do something with it."

"That was my idea," said Montague. "I have broached it to one."

"Indeed?" said the Colonel. "Possibly that is where my offer came from. Who was it?"

"It was Jim Hegan," said Montague.

"Oh!" said the Colonel. "But, of course," he added, "Hegan would do his negotiating through an agent."

"Let me give you my card," said the Colonel, after a pause. "It is possible that I may be able to interest someone in the matter myself. I have friends who believe in the future of the South. How many shares do you suppose you could get me, and what do you suppose they would cost?"

Montague got out a pencil and paper, and proceeded to recall as well as he could the location of the various holdings of Northern Mississippi. He and his new acquaintance became quite engrossed in the subject, and they talked it out from many points of view. By the time that Montague's friend arrived, the Colonel was in possession of all the facts, and he promised that he would write in a very few days.

And then, after dinner, Montague went upstairs and joined his mother. "I met an old friend of father's this evening," he said.

"Who was it?" she asked.

"Colonel Cole," he said, and Mrs. Montague looked blank.

"Colonel Cole?" she repeated.

"Yes, that was the name," said Montague. "Here is his card," and he took it out. "Henry W. Cole, Seattle, Washington," it read.

"But I never heard of him," said Mrs. Montague.

"Never heard of him!" exclaimed Montague. "Why, he has been at the house a dozen times, and he knew father and Cousin Lee and Judge Dupree and everyone."

But Mrs. Montague only shook her head. "He may have been at the house," she said, "but I am sure that I was never introduced to him."

Montague thought that it was strange, but he would never have given further thought to the matter had it not been for something which occurred the next morning. He went to the office rather early, on account of important work which he had to get ready. He was the first to arrive, and he found the scrub-woman who cleaned the office just taking her departure.

It had never occurred to Montague before that such a person existed; and he turned in some surprise when she spoke to him.

"I beg pardon, sir," she said. "But there is something I have to tell you."

"What is it?" said he.

"There is someone trying to find out about you," said the woman.

"What do you mean?" he asked, in perplexity.

"Begging your pardon, sir," said the woman, "but there was a man came here this morning, very early, and he offered me money, sir, and he wanted me to save him all the papers that I took out of your scrap-basket, sir."

Montague caught his breath. "Papers out of my scrap-basket!" he gasped.

"Yes, sir," said the woman. "It is done now and then, sir—we learn of such things, you know. And we are poor women—they don't pay us very well. But you are a gentleman, sir, and I told him I would have nothing to do with it."

"What sort of a looking man was he?" Montague demanded.

"He was a dark chap, sir," said the other, "a sort of Jew like. He will maybe came back again."

Montague took out his purse and gave the woman a bill; and she stammered her thanks and went off with her pail and broom.

He shut the door and went and sat down at his desk, and stared in front of him, gasping, "My God!"

Then suddenly he struck his knee with an exclamation of rage. "I told him everything that I knew! Everything! He hardly had to ask me a question!"

But then, again, wonder drowned every other emotion in him. "What in the world can he have wanted to know? And who sent him? What can it mean?"

He went back over his talk with the old gentleman from Seattle, trying to recall exactly what he had told, and what use the other could have made of the information. But he could not think very steadily, for his mind kept jumping back to the thought of Jim Hegan.

There could be but one explanation of all this. Jim Hegan had set detectives upon him! Nobody else knew anything about the Northern Mississippi Railroad, or wanted to know about it.

Jim Hegan! And Montague had met him socially at an entertainment—at Mrs. de Graffenried's! He had met him as one gentleman meets another, had shaken hands with him, had gone and talked with him freely and frankly! And then Hegan had sent a detective to worm his secrets from him, and had even tried to get at the contents of his trash-basket!

There was only one resort that Montague could think of, in a case so perplexing. He sat down and wrote a note to his friend Major Venable, at the Millionaires' Club, saying that he was coming there to dinner, and would like to have the Major's company. And two or three hours later, when sufficient time had elapsed for the Major to have had his shave and his coffee and his morning newspaper, he rang for a messenger and sent the note.

The Major's reply was prompt. He had no engagement, and his stores of information and advice were at Montague's service. But his gout was bad, and his temper atrocious, and Montague must be warned in advance that his doctors permitted him neither mushrooms nor meat.

It always seemed to Montague that it could not be possible for a human face to wear a brighter shade of purple than the Major's; yet every time he met him, it seemed to him that the purple was a shade brighter. And it spread farther with every step the Major took. He growled and grumbled, and swore tremendous oaths under his breath, and the way the head-waiter and all his assistants scurried about the dining-room of the Club was a joy to the beholder.

Montague waited until the old gentleman had obtained his usual dry Martini, and until he had solved the problem of satisfying his appetite and his doctor. And then he told of his extraordinary experience.

"I felt sure that you could explain it, if anybody could," said he.

"But what is there to explain?" asked the other. "It simply means that Jim Hegan is interested in your railroad. What more could you want?"

"But he sent a detective after me!" gasped Montague.

"But that's all right," said the Major. "It is done every day. There are half-a-dozen big agencies that do nothing else. You are lucky if he hasn't had your telephone tapped, and read your telegrams and mail before you saw them."

Montague stared at him aghast. "A man like Jim Hegan!" he exclaimed. "And to a friend."

"A friend?" said the Major. "Pshaw! A man doesn't do business with friends. And, besides, Jim Hegan probably never knew anything about it. He turned the whole matter over to some subordinate, and told him to look it up, and he'll give never another thought to it until the facts are laid upon his desk. Some one of his men set to work, and he was a little clumsy about it— that's all."

"But why did he want to know about all my family affairs?"

"Why, he wanted to know how you were situated," said the other—"how badly you wanted to sell the stock. So when he came to do business with you, he'd have you where he wanted you, and he'd probably get fifty per cent off the price because of it. You'll be lucky if he doesn't have a few loans called on you at your bank."

The Major sat watching Montague, smiling at his *naïveté*. "Where did you say this road was?" he asked. "In Mississippi?"

"Yes," said Montague.

"I was wondering about it," said the other. "It is not likely that it's Jim Hegan at all. I don't believe anybody could get him to take an interest in Southern railroads. He has probably mentioned it to someone else. What's your road good for, anyway?"

"We had a plan to extend it," said Montague.

"It would take but one or two million to carry it to the main works of the Mississippi Steel Company."

The Major gave a start. "The Mississippi Steel Company!" he exclaimed.

"Yes," said Montague.

"Oh, my God!" cried the other.

"What's the matter?"

"Why in the world did you take a matter like that to Jim Hegan?" demanded Major Venable.

"I took it to him because I knew him," said Montague.

"But one doesn't take things to people because one knows them," said the Major. "One takes them to the right people. If Jim Hegan could have his way, he would wipe the Mississippi Steel Company off the map of the United States."

"What do you mean?"

"Don't you know," said the Major, "that Mississippi Steel is the chief competitor of the Trust? And old Dan Waterman organized the Steel Trust, and watches it all the time."

"But what's that got to do with Hegan?"

"Simply that Jim Hegan works with Waterman in everything."

Montague stared in dismay. "I see," he said.

"Of course!" said the Major. "My dear fellow, why don't you come to me before you do things like that? You should have gone to the Mississippi Steel people; and you should have gone quietly, and to the men at the top. For all you can tell, you may have a really big proposition that's been overlooked in the shuffle. What was that you said about the survey?"

And Montague told in detail the story of the aborted plan for an extension, and of his hunting trip, and what he had learned on it.

"Of course," said the Major, "you are in the heart of the thing right now. The Steel people balked your plan."

"How do you mean?" asked the other.

"They bought up the survey. And they've probably controlled your railroad ever since, and kept it down."

"But that's impossible! They've nothing to do with it."

"Bah!" said the Major. "How could you know?"

"I know the president," said Montague. "He's an old friend of the family's."

"Yes," was the reply. "But suppose they have a mortgage on his business?"

"But why not buy the road and be done with it?" added Montague, in perplexity.

The other laughed. "I am reminded of a famous saying of Wyman's—'Why should I buy stock when I can buy directors?'"

"It's those same people who are watching you now," he continued, after a pause. "Probably they think it is some move of the other side, and they are trying to run the thing down."

"Who owns the Mississippi Steel Company?" asked Montague.

"I don't know," said the Major. "I fancy that Wyman must have come into it somehow. Didn't you notice in the papers the other day that the contracts for furnishing rails for all his three transcontinental railroads had gone to the Mississippi Steel Company?"

"Sure enough!" exclaimed Montague.

"You see!" said the Major, with a chuckle. "You have jumped right into the middle of the frog pond, and the Lord only knows what a ruction you have stirred up! Just think of the situation for a moment. The Steel Trust is over-capitalized two hundred per cent. Because of the tariff it is able to sell its product at home for fifty per cent more than it charges abroad; and even so, it has to keep cutting its dividends! Its common stock is down to ten. It is cutting expenses on every hand, and of course it's turning out a rotten product. And now along comes Wyman, the one man in Wall Street who dares to shake his fist at old Dan Waterman; and he gives the newspapers all the facts about the bad steel rails that are causing smash-ups on his roads; and he turns all his contracts over to the Mississippi Steel Company, which is underselling the Trust. The company is swamped with orders, and its plants are running day and night. And then along comes a guileless young fool with a little dinky railroad which he wants to run into the Company's back-door yard; and he takes the proposition to Jim Hegan!"

The Major arrived at his climax in a state of suppressed emotion, which culminated in a chuckle, which shook his rubicund visage and brought a series of twitches to his aching toe. As for Montague, he was duly humbled.

"What would you do now?" he asked, after a pause.

"I don't see that there's anything to do," said the Major, "except to hold on tight to your stock. Perhaps if you go on talking out loud about your extension, some of the Steel people will buy you out at your own price."

"I gave them a scare, anyhow," said Montague, laughing.

"I can wager one thing," said the other. "There has been a fine shaking up in somebody's office down town! There's a man who comes here every night, who's probably heard of it. That's Will Roberts."

And the Major looked about the dining-room. "Here he comes now," he said.

At the farther end of the room there had entered a tall, dark-haired man, with a keen expression and a brisk step. "Roberts the Silent," said the Major. "Let's have a try at him." And as the man passed near, he hailed him. "Hello! Roberts, where are you going? Let me introduce my friend, Mr. Allan Montague."

The man looked at Montague. "Good evening, sir," he said. "How are you, Venable?"

"Couldn't be worse, thank you," said the Major. "How are things with you on the Street?"

"Dull, very dull," said Roberts as he passed on. "Matters look bad, I'm afraid. Too many people making money rapidly."

The Major chuckled. "A fine sentiment," he said, when Roberts had passed out of hearing—"from a man who has made sixty millions in the last ten years!"

"It did not appear that he had ever heard of me," said Montague.

"Oh, trust him for that!" said the Major. "He might have been planning to have your throat cut to-night, but you wouldn't have seen him turn an eyelid. He is that sort; he's made of steel himself, I believe."

He paused, and then went on, in a reminiscent mood, "You've read of the great strike, I suppose? It was Roberts put that job through. He made himself the worst-hated man in the country—try—Gad! how the newspapers and the politicians used to rage at him! But he stood his ground—he would win that strike or die in the attempt. And he very nearly did both, you know. An

Anarchist came to his office and shot him twice; but he got the fellow down and nearly choked the life out of him, and he ran the strike on his sick-bed, and two weeks later he was back in his office again."

And now the Major's store-rooms of gossip were unlocked. He told Montague about the kings of Steel, and about the men they had hated and the women they had loved, and about the inmost affairs and secrets of their lives. William H. Roberts had begun his career in the service of the great iron-master, whose deadly rival he had afterwards become; and now he lived but to dispute that rival's claims to glory. Let the rival build a library, Roberts would build two. Let the rival put up a great office building, Roberts would buy all the land about it, and put up half a dozen, and completely shut out its light. And day and night "Roberts the Silent" was plotting and planning, and some day he would be the master of the Steel Trust, and his rival would be nowhere.

"They are lively chaps, the Steel crowd," said the Major, chuckling. "You will have to keep your eyes open when you do business with them."

"What would you advise me to do?" asked the other, smiling. "Set detectives after them?"

"Why not?" asked the Major seriously. "Why not find out who sent that Colonel Cole to see you? And find out how badly he needs your little railroad, and make him pay for it accordingly."

"That is not *quite* in my line," said Montague.

"It's time you were learning," said the Major. "I can start you. I know a detective whom you can trust.—At any rate," he added cautiously, "I don't know that he's ever played me false."

Montague sat for a while in thought. "You said something about their getting after one's telephone," he observed. "Did you really mean that?"

"Of course," said the other.

"Do you mean to tell me that they could find out what goes over my 'phone?"

"I mean to tell you," was the reply, "that for two hundred and fifty dollars I can get you a stenographic report of every word

that you say over your 'phone for twenty-four hours, and of
every word that anybody says to you."

"That sounds incredible!" said Montague. "Who does it?"

"Wire-tappers. It's dangerous work, but the pay is big. I have
a friend who once upon a time was putting through a deal in
which the telephone company was interested, and they trans-
ferred his wire to another branch, and he finished up his business before the other side got on to the trick. To this day you'll
notice that his telephone is 'Spring,' though every other 'phone
in the neighbourhood is 'John.'"

"And mail, too?" asked Montague.

"Mail!" echoed the Major. "What's easier than that? You can
hold up a man's mail for twenty-four hours and take a photograph of every letter. You can do the same with every letter that
he mails, unless he is very careful. He can be followed, you
understand, and every time he drops a letter, a blue or yellow
envelope is dropped on top—for a signal to the post-office
people."

"But then, so many persons would have to know about that."

"Nothing of the kind. That's a regular branch of the post-
office work. There are Secret Service men who are watching
criminals that way all the time. And what could be easier than to
pay one of them, and to have your enemy listed with the sus-
pects?"

The Major smiled in amusement. It always gave him delight
to witness Montague's consternation over his pictures of the
city's corruption.

"There are things even stranger than that," he said. "I can
introduce you to a man, who's in this room now, who was fighting the Ship-building swindle, and he got hold of a lot of important papers, and he took them to his office, and sat by while his
clerks made thirty-two copies of them. And he put the originals
and thirty-one of the copies in thirty-two different safe-deposit
vaults in the city, and took the other copy to his home in a valise.
And that night burglars broke in, and the valise was missing. The
next day he wrote to the people he was fighting, 'I was going to
send you a copy of the papers which have come into my possession, but as you already have a copy, I will simply proceed to

outline my proposition.' And that was all. They settled for a million or two."

The Major paused a moment and looked across the dining-room. "There goes Dick Sanderson," he said, pointing to a dapper young man with a handsome, smooth-shaven face. "He represents the New Jersey Southern Railroad. And one day another lawyer who met him at dinner remarked, 'I am going to bring a stockholders' suit against your road to-morrow.' He went on to outline the case, which was a big one. Sanderson said nothing, but he went out and telephoned to their agent in Trenton, and the next morning a Bill went through both houses of the Legislature providing a statute of limitations that outlawed the case. The man who was the victim of that trick is now the Governor of New York State, and if you ever meet him, you can ask him about it."

There was a pause for a while; then suddenly the Major remarked, "Oh, by the way, this beautiful widow you have brought up from Mississippi—Mrs. Taylor—is that the name?"

"That's it," said Montague.

"I hear that Stanley Ryder has taken quite a fancy to her," said the other.

A grave look came upon Montague's face. "I am sorry, indeed, that you have heard it," he said.

"Why," said the other, "that's all right. He will give her a good time."

"Lucy is new to New York," said Montague. "I don't think she quite realizes the sort of man that Ryder is."

The Major thought for a moment, then suddenly began to laugh. "It might be just as well for her to be careful," he said. "I happened to think of it—they say that Mrs. Stanley is getting ready to free herself from the matrimonial bond; and if your fascinating widow doesn't want to get into the newspapers, she had better be a little careful with her favours."

CHAPTER IV

Two or three days after this Montague met Jim Hegan at a directors' meeting. He watched him closely, but Hegan gave no sign of constraint. He was courteous and serene as ever. "By the way, Mr. Montague," he said, "I mentioned that railroad matter to a friend who is interested. You may hear from him in a few days."

"I am obliged to you," said the other, and that was all.

The next day was Sunday, and Montague came to take Lucy to church, and told her of this remark. He did not tell her about the episode with Colonel Cole, for he thought there was no use disturbing her.

She, for her part, had other matters to talk about. "By the way, Allan," she said, "I presume you know that the coaching parade is to-morrow."

"Yes," said he.

"Mr. Ryder has offered me a seat on his coach," said Lucy.— "I suppose you are going to be angry with me," she added quickly, seeing his frown.

"You said you would go?" he asked.

"Yes," said Lucy. "I did not think it would be any harm. It is such a public matter——"

"A public matter!" exclaimed Montague. "I should think so! To sit up on top of a coach for the crowds to stare at, and for thirty or forty newspaper reporters to take snapshots of! And to have yourself blazoned as the fascinating young widow from Mississippi who was one of Stanley Ryder's party, and then to have all Society looking at the picture and winking and making remarks about it!"

"You take such a cynical view of everything," protested Lucy. "How can people help it if the crowds will stare, and if the newspapers will take pictures? Surely one cannot give up the pleasure of going for a drive——"

"Oh, pshaw, Lucy!" said Montague. "You have too much sense to talk like that. If you want to drive, go ahead and drive. But when a lot of people get together and pay ten or twenty thousand dollars apiece for fancy coaches and horses, and then appoint a day and send out notice to the whole city, and dress themselves up in fancy costumes and go out and make a public parade of themselves, they have no right to talk about driving for pleasure."

"Well," said she dubiously, "it's nice to be noticed."

"It is for those who like it," said he; "and if a woman chooses to set out on a publicity campaign, and run a press bureau, and make herself a public character, why, that's her privilege. But for Heaven's sake let her drop the sickly pretence that she is only driving beautiful horses, or listening to music, or entertaining her friends. I suppose a Society woman has as much right to advertise her personality as a politician or a manufacturer of pills; all I object to is the sham of it, the everlasting twaddle about her love of privacy. Take Mrs. Winnie Duval, for instance. You would think to hear her that her one ideal in life was to be a simple shepherdess and to raise flowers; but, as a matter of fact, she keeps a scrap-album, and if a week passes when the newspapers do not have some paragraphs about her doings, she begins to get restless."

Lucy broke into a laugh. "I was at Mrs. Robbie Walling's last night," she said. "She was talking about the crowds at the opera, and she said she was going to withdraw to some place where she wouldn't have to see such mobs of ugly people."

"Yes," said he. "But you can't tell me anything about Mrs. Robbie Walling. I have been there. There's nothing that lady does from the time she opens her eyes in the morning until the time she goes to bed the next morning that she would ever care to do if it were not for the mobs of ugly people looking on."

—"You seem to be going everywhere," said Montague, after a pause.

"Oh, I guess I'm a success," said Lucy. "I am certainly having a gorgeous time. I never saw so many beautiful houses or such dazzling costumes in my life."

"It's very fine," said Montague. "But take it slowly and make it last. When one has got used to it, the life seems rather dull and grey."

"I am invited to the Wymans' to-night," said Lucy—"to play bridge. Fancy giving a bridge-party on Sunday night!"

Montague shrugged his shoulders. "*Cosí fan tutti,*" he said.

"What do you make of Betty Wyman?" asked the other.

"She is having a good time," said he. "I don't think she has much conscience about it."

"Is she very much in love with Ollie?" she asked.

"I don't know," he said. "I can't make them out. It doesn't seem to trouble them very much."

This was after church while they were strolling down the Avenue, gazing at the procession of new spring costumes.— "Who is that stately creature you just bowed to?" inquired Lucy.

"That?" said Montague. "That is Miss Hegan—Jim Hegan's daughter."

"Oh!" said Lucy. "I remember—Betty Wyman told me about her."

"Nothing very good, I imagine," said Montague, with a smile.

"It was interesting," said Lucy. "Fancy having a father with a hundred millions, and talking about going in for settlement work!"

"Well," he answered, "I told you one could get tired of the splurge."

Lucy looked at him quizzically. "I should think that kind of a girl would rather appeal to you," she said.

"I would like to know her very much," said he, "but she didn't seem to like me."

"Not like you!" cried the other. "Why, how perfectly outrageous!"

"It was not her fault," said Montague, smiling; "I am afraid I got myself a bad reputation."

"Oh, you mean about Mrs. Winnie!" exclaimed Lucy.

"Yes," said he, "that's it."

"I wish you would tell me about it," said she.

"There is nothing much to tell. Mrs. Winnie proceeded to take me up and make a social success of me, and I was fool enough to come when she invited me. Then the first thing I knew, all the gossips were wagging their tongues."

"That didn't do you any harm, did it?" asked Lucy.

"Not particularly," said he, shrugging his shoulders. "Only here is a woman whom I would have liked to know, and I don't know her. That's all."

Lucy gave him a sly glance. "You need a sister," she said, smiling. "Somebody to fight for you!"

According to Jim Hegan's prediction, it was not long before Montague received an offer. It came from a firm of lawyers of whom he had never heard. "We understand," ran the letter, "that you have a block of five thousand shares of the stock of the Northern Mississippi Railroad. We have a client on whose behalf we are authorized to offer you fifty thousand dollars cash for these shares. Will you kindly consult with your client, and advise us at your earliest convenience?"

He called up Lucy on the 'phone and told her that the offer had come.

"How much?" she asked eagerly.

"It is not satisfactory," he said. "But I would rather not discuss the matter over the 'phone. How can I arrange to see you?"

"Can't you send me up the letter by a messenger?" she asked.

"I could," said Montague, "but I would like to talk with you about it; and also I have that mortgage, and the other papers for you to sign. There are some things to be explained about these, also. Couldn't you come to my office this morning?"

"I would, Allan," she said, "but I have just made a most important engagement, and I don't know what to do about it."

"Couldn't it be postponed?" he asked.

"No," she said. "It's an invitation to join a party on Mr. Waterman's new yacht."

"The *Brünnhilde!*" exclaimed Montague. "You don't say so!"

"Yes, and I hate to miss it," said she.

"How long shall you be gone?" he asked.

"I shall be back some time this evening," she answered. "We are going up the Sound. The yacht has just been put into commission, you know."

"Where is she lying?"

"Off the Battery. I am to be on board in an hour, and I was just about to start. Couldn't you possibly meet me there?"

"Yes," said Montague. "I will come over. I suppose they will wait a few minutes."

"I am half dying to know about the offer," said Lucy.

Montague had a couple of callers, which delayed him somewhat; finally he jumped into a cab and drove to the Battery.

Here, in the neighbourhood of Castle Garden, was a sheltered place popularly known as the "Millionaires' Basin," being the favourite anchorage of the private yachts of the "Wall Street flotilla." At this time of the year most of the great men had already moved out to their country places, and those of them who lived on the Hudson or up the Sound would come to their offices in vessels of every size, from racing motor-boats to huge private steamships. They would have their breakfasts served on board, and would have their secretaries and their mail.

Many of these yachts were floating palaces of incredible magnificence; one, upon which Montague had been a guest, had a glass-domed library extending entirely around its upper deck. This one was the property of the Lester Todds, and the main purpose it served was to carry them upon their various hunting trips; its equipment included such luxuries as a French laundry, a model dairy and poultry-yard, an ice-machine, and a shooting-gallery.

And here lay the *Brünnhilde*, the wonderful new toy of old Waterman. Montague knew all about her, for she had just been completed that spring, and not a newspaper in the Metropolis but had had her picture, and full particulars about her cost. Waterman had purchased her from the King of Belgium, who had thought she was everything the soul of a monarch could desire. Great had been his consternation when he learned that the new owner had given orders to strip her down to the bare steel hull and refit and refurnish her. The saloon was now done with Louis Quinze decorations, said the newspapers. Its walls were panelled in satinwood and inlaid walnut, and underfoot were velvet carpets twelve feet wide and woven without seam. Its closets were automatically lighted, and opened at the touch of a button; even the drawers of its bureaus were upon ball-bearings. The owner's private bedroom measured the entire width of the vessel, twenty-eight feet, and opened upon a Roman bath of white marble.

Such was the *Brünnhilde*. Montague looked about him for one of the yacht's launches, but he could not find any, so he hailed a boatman and had himself rowed out. A man in uniform met him at the steps. "Is Mrs. Taylor on board?" he asked.

"She is," the other answered. "Is this Mr. Montague? She left word for you."

Montague had begun to ascend; but half a second later he stopped short in consternation.

Through one of the portholes of the vessel he heard distinctly a muffled cry—

"Help! help!"

And he recognized the voice. It was Lucy's!

CHAPTER V

Montague hesitated only an instant. He sprang up to the deck. "Where is Mrs. Taylor?" he cried.

"She went below, sir," said the man, hesitating; but Montague sprang past him and down the companionway.

At the foot of the stairs he found himself in a broad entrance-hall, lighted by a glass dome above. He sprang toward a door which opened in the direction of the cry he had heard, and shouted aloud, "Lucy! Lucy!" He heard her answer beyond the doorway, and he seized the knob and tried it. The door was locked.

"Open the door!" he shouted.

There was no sound. "Open the door!" he called again, "or I'll break it down."

Suiting his action to the word, he flung his weight upon it. The barrier cracked; and then suddenly he heard a man's voice. "All right. Wait."

Someone fumbled at the knob; and Montague stood crouching and watching breathlessly, prepared for anything. The door opened, and he found himself confronted by Dan Waterman.

Montague recoiled a step in consternation; and the other strode out, and without a word went past him down the hall. There was just time enough for Montague to receive one look— of the most furious rage that he had ever seen upon a human face.

He rushed into the room. Lucy was standing at the farther end, leaning upon a table to support herself. Her clothing was in disarray, and her hair was falling about her ears; her face was flushed, and she was panting in great agitation.

"Lucy!" he gasped, running to her. She caught at his arm to steady herself.

"What is the matter?" he cried. She turned her face away, making not a sound.

For a minute or so he stood staring at her. Then she whispered, "Quick! let us go from here!"

And with a sudden movement of her hands, she swept her hair back from her forehead, and straightened her clothing, and started to the door, leaning upon her friend.

They went up to the deck, where the officer was still standing in perplexity.

"Mrs. Taylor wishes to go ashore," said Montague. "Will you get us a boat?"

"The launch will be back in a few minutes, sir——" the man began.

"We wish to go at once," said Montague. "Will you let us have one of those row-boats? Otherwise I shall hail that tug."

The man hesitated but a moment. Montague's voice was determined, and so he turned and gave orders to lower a small boat.

In the meantime, Lucy stood, breathing heavily, and gazing about her nervously. When at last they had left the yacht, he heard her sigh with relief.

They sat in silence until she had stepped upon the landing. Then she said, "Get me a cab, Allan."

He led her to the street and hailed a vehicle. When they were seated, Lucy sank back with a gasp. "Please don't ask me to talk, Allan," she said. And she made not another sound during the long drive to the hotel.

"Is there anything I can do for you?" he said, after he had seen her safely to her apartment.

"No," she answered. "I am all right. Wait for me."

She retired to her dressing-room, and when she came back, all traces of her excitement had been removed. Then she seated herself in a chair opposite Montague and gazed at him.

"Allan," she began, "I have been trying to think. What can I do to that man?"

"I am sure I don't know," he answered.

"Why, I can hardly believe that this is New York," she gasped. "I feel as though I had got back into the Middle Ages!"

"You forget, Lucy," he replied, "that I don't know what happened."

Again she fell silent. They sat staring at each other, and then suddenly she leaned back in her chair and began to laugh. Once she had started, burst after burst of merriment swept over her. "I try to stay angry, Allan!" she gasped. "It seems as if I ought to. But, honestly, it was perfectly absurd!"

"I am sure you'd much better laugh than cry," said he.

"I will tell you about it, Allan," the girl went on. "I know I shall have to tell somebody, or I shall simply explode. You will have to advise me about it, for I was never more bewildered in my life."

"Go ahead," said he. "Begin at the beginning."

"I told you how I met Waterman at his art gallery," said Lucy. "Mr. David Alden took me, and the old man was so polite, and so dignified—why, I never had the slightest idea! And then he wrote me a little note—in his own hand, mind you—inviting me to be one of a party for the first trip of the *Brünnhilde*. Of course, I thought it was all right. I told you I was going, you know, and you didn't have any objections either.

"I went down there, and the launch met me and took me on board, and a steward took me down into that room and left me, and a second later the old man himself came in. And he shut the door behind him and locked it!

"'How do you do, Mrs. Taylor?' he said, and before I had a chance even to open my mouth and reply, he came to me and calmly put his arms around me.

"You can fancy my feelings. I was simply paralyzed!

"'Mr. Waterman?' I gasped.

"I didn't hear what he said; I was almost dazed with anger and fright. I remember I cried several times, 'Let me go!' but he paid not the slightest attention to me. He just held me tight in his arms.

"Finally I got myself together a little. I didn't want to bite and scratch like a kitchen wench. I tried to speak calmly.

"'Mr. Waterman,' I said, 'I want you to release me.'

"'I love you,' he said.

"'But I don't love you,' I protested. I remember thinking even then how absurd it sounded. I can't think of anything that wouldn't have sounded absurd in such a situation.

"'You will learn to love me,' he said. 'Many women have.'

"'I am not that sort of a woman,' I said. 'I tell you, you have made a mistake. Let me go.'

"'I want you,' he said. 'And when I want a thing, I get it. I never take any refusal—understand that. You don't realize the situation. It will be no disgrace to you. Women think it an honour to have me love them. Think what I can do for you. You can have anything you want. You can go anywhere you wish. I will never stint you.'

"I remember his going on like that for some time. And fancy, there I was! I might as well have been in the grip of a bear. You would not think it, you know, but he is terribly strong. I could not move. I could hardly think. I was suffocated, and all the time I could feel his breath on my face, and he was glaring into my eyes like some terrible wild beast.

"'Mr. Waterman,' I protested, 'I am not used to being treated in this way.'

"'I know, I know,' he said. 'If you were, I should not want you. But I am different from other men. Think of it—think of all that I have on my hands. I have no time to make love to women. But I love you. I loved you the minute I saw you. Is not that enough? What more can you ask?'

"'You have brought me here under false pretences,' I cried. 'You have taken cowardly advantage of me. If you have a spark of decency in you, you should be ashamed of yourself.'

"'Tut, tut,' he said, 'don't talk that kind of nonsense. You know the world. You are no spring chicken.'—Yes, he did, Allan—I remember that very phrase. And it made me so furious—you can't imagine! I tried to get away again, but the more I struggled, the more it seemed to enrage him. I was positively terrified. You know, I don't believe there was another person on board that yacht except his servants.

"'Mr. Waterman,' I cried, 'I tell you to take your hands off me. If you don't, I will make a disturbance. I will scream.'

"'It won't do you any good,' he said savagely.

"'But what do you want me to *do?*'" I protested.

"'I want you to love me,' he said.

"And then I began to struggle again. I shouted once or twice—I am not sure—and then he clapped his hand over my mouth. Then I began to fight for my life. I really believe I would have scratched the old creature's eyes out if he had not heard you out in the hall. When you called my name, he dropped me and sprang back. I never saw such furious hatred on a man's countenance in my life.

"When I answered you, I tried to run to the door, but he stood in my way.

"'I will follow you!' he whispered. 'Do you understand me? I will never give you up!'

"And then you flung yourself against the door, and he turned and opened it and went out."

Lucy had turned scarlet over the recalling of the scene, and she was breathing quickly in her agitation. Montague sat staring in front of him, without a sound.

"Did you ever hear of anything like that in your life before?" she asked.

"Yes," said he gravely, "I am sorry to say that I have heard of it several times. I have heard of things even worse."

"But what am I to do?" she cried. "Surely a man can't behave like that with impunity."

Montague said nothing.

"He is a monster!" cried Lucy. "I ought to have him put in jail."

Montague shook his head. "You couldn't do that," he said.

"I couldn't!" exclaimed the other. "Why not?"

"You couldn't prove it," said Montague.

"It would be your word against his, and they would take his every time. You can't go and have Dan Waterman arrested as you could any ordinary man. And think of the notoriety it would mean!"

"I would like to expose him," protested Lucy. "It would serve him right!"

"It would not do him the least harm in the world," said Montague. "I can speak quite positively there, for I have seen it tried. You couldn't get a newspaper in New York to publish that story. All that you could do would be to have yourself blazoned as an adventuress."

Lucy was staring, with clenched hands. "Why, I might as well be living in Turkey," she cried.

"Very nearly," said he. "There's an old man in this town who has spent his lifetime lending money and hoarding it; he has something like eighty or a hundred millions now, I believe, and once every six months or so you will read in the newspapers that some woman has made an attempt to blackmail him. That is because he does to every pretty girl who comes into his office just exactly what old Waterman did to you; and those who are arrested for blackmail are simply the ones who are so unwise as to make a disturbance."

"You see, Lucy," continued Montague, after a pause, "you must realize the situation. This man is a god in New York. He controls all the avenues of wealth; he can make or break any person he chooses. It is really the truth—I believe he could ruin any man in the city whom he chose to set out after. He can have anything that he wants done, so far as the police are concerned. It is simply a matter of paying them. And he is accustomed to rule in everything; his lightest whim is law. If he wants a thing, he buys it, and that is his attitude towards women. He is used to being treated as a master; women seek him, and vie for his favour. If you had been able to hold it, you might have had a million-dollar palace on Riverside Drive, or a cottage with a million-dollar pier at Newport. You might have had *carte-blanche* at all the shops, and all the yachting trips and private trains that you wanted. That is all that other women want, and he could not understand what more you could want." Montague paused.

"Is that the way he spends his money?" Lucy asked.

"He buys everything he takes a fancy to," said Montague. "They say he spends five thousand dollars a day. One of the stories they tell in the clubs is that he loved the wife of a physician, and he gave a million dollars to found a hospital, and one of the conditions of the endowment was that this physician should go abroad for three years and study all the hospitals of Europe."

Lucy sat buried in thought. "Allan," she asked suddenly, "what do you suppose he meant by saying he would follow me? What could he do?"

"I don't know," said Allan, "it is something which we shall have to think over very carefully."

"He made a remark to me that I thought was very strange," she said. "I just happened to recall it. He said, 'You have no money. You cannot keep up the pace in New York. What you own is worth nothing.' Do you suppose, Allan, that he can know anything about my affairs?"

Montague was staring at her in consternation. "Lucy!" he exclaimed.

"What is it?" she cried.

"Nothing," he said; and he added to himself, "No, it is absurd. It could not be." The idea that it could have been Dan Waterman who had set the detectives to follow him seemed too grotesque for consideration. "It was nothing but a chance shot," he said to Lucy, "but you must be careful. He is a dangerous man."

"And I am powerless to punish him!" whispered Lucy, after a pause.

"It seems to me," said Montague, "that you are very well out of it. You will know better next time; and as for punishing him, I fancy that Nature will attend to that. He is getting old, you know; and they say he is morose and wretched."

"But, Allan!" protested Lucy. "I can't help thinking what would have happened to me if you had not come on board! I can't help thinking about other women who must have been caught in such a trap. Why, Allan, I would have been equally helpless—no matter what he had done!"

"I am afraid so," said he gravely. "Many a woman has discovered it, I imagine. I understand how you feel, but what can you do about it? You can't punish men like Waterman. You can't punish them for anything they do, whether it is monopolizing a necessity of life and starving thousands of people to death, or whether it is an attack upon a defenceless woman. There are rich men in this city who make it their diversion to answer advertisements and decoy young girls. A stenographer in my office told me that she had had over twenty positions in one year, and that she had left every one because some man in the office had approached her."

He paused for a moment. "You see," he added, "I have been finding out these things. You thought I was unreasonable, but I know what your dangers are. You are a stranger here; you have no friends and no influence, and so you will always be the one to suffer. I don't mean merely in a case like this, where it comes to the police and the newspapers; I mean in social matters— where it is a question of your reputation, of the interpretation which people will place upon your actions. They have their wealth and their prestige and their privileges, and they stand at bay. They are perfectly willing to give a stranger a good time, if the stranger has a pretty face and a lively wit to entertain them; but when you come to trespass, or to threaten their power, then you find out how they can hate you, and how mercilessly they will slander and ruin you!"

CHAPTER VI

Lucy's adventure had so taken up the attention of them both that they had forgotten all about the matter of the stock. Afterwards, however, Montague mentioned it, and Lucy exclaimed indignantly at the smallness of the offer.

"That is only ten cents on the dollar!" she cried. "You surely would not advise me to sell for that!"

"No, I should not," he answered. "I should reject the offer. It might be well, however, to set a price for them to consider."

They had talked this matter over before, and had agreed upon a hundred and eighty thousand dollars. "I think it will be best to state that figure," he said, "and give them to understand that it is final. I imagine they would expect to bargain, but I am not much of a hand at that, and would prefer to say what I mean and stick by it."

"Very well!" said Lucy, "you use your own judgment."

There was a pause; then Montague, seeing the look on Lucy's face, started to his feet. "It won't do you any good to think about to-day's mishap," he said. "Let's start over again, and not make any more mistakes. Come with me this evening. I have some friends who have been begging me to bring you around ever since you came."

"Who are they?" asked Lucy.

"General Prentice and his wife. Do you know of them?"

"I have heard Mr. Ryder speak of Prentice the banker. Is that the one you mean?"

"Yes," said Montague—"the president of the Trust Company of the Republic. He was an old comrade of my father's, and they were the first people I met here in New York. I have got to know them very well since. I told them I would bring you up to dinner sometime, and I will telephone them, if you say so. I don't think it's a good idea for you to sit here by yourself and think about Dan Waterman."

"Oh, I don't mind it now," said Lucy. "But I will go with you, if you like."

They went to the Prentices'. There were the General himself, and Mrs. Prentice, and their two daughters, one of whom was a student in college, and the other a violinist of considerable talent. General Prentice was now over seventy, and his beard was snow-white, but he still had the erect carriage and the commanding presence of a soldier. Mrs. Prentice Montague had first met one evening when he had been their guest at the opera, and she had impressed him as a lady with a great many diamonds, who talked to him about other people while he was trying to listen to the music. But she was, as Lucy phrased it afterwards, "a motherly soul, when one got underneath her warpaint." She was always inviting Montague to her home and introducing him to people whom she thought would be of assistance to him.

Also there came that evening young Harry Curtiss, the General's nephew. Montague had never met him before, but he knew him as a junior partner in the firm of William E. Davenant, the famous corporation lawyer—the man whom Montague had found opposed to him in his suit against the Fidelity Insurance Company. Harry Curtiss, whom Montague was to know quite well before long, was a handsome fellow, with frank and winning manners. He had met Alice Montague at an affair a week or so ago, and he sent word that he was coming to see her.

After dinner they sat and smoked, and talked about the condition of the market. It was a time of great agitation in Wall Street. There had been a violent slump in stocks, and matters seemed to be going from bad to worse.

"They say that Wyman has got caught," said Curtiss, repeating one of the wild tales of the "Street." "I was talking with one of his brokers yesterday."

"Wyman is not an easy man to catch," said the General. "His own brokers are often the last men to know his real situation. There is good reason to believe that some of the big insiders are loaded up, for the public is very uneasy, as you know; but with the situation as it is just now in Wall Street, you can't tell anything. The men who are really on the inside have matters so completely in their own hands that they are practically omnipotent."

"You mean that you think this slump may be the result of manipulation?" asked Montague wonderingly.

"Why not?" asked the General.

"It seems to be such a widespread movement," said Montague. "It seems incredible that any one man could cause such an upset."

"It is not one man," said the General; "it is a group of men. I don't say that it's true, mind you. I wouldn't be at liberty to say it even if I knew it; but there are certain things that I have seen, and I have my suspicions of others. And you must realize that half a dozen men now control about ninety per cent of the banks of this city."

"Things will get worse before they get any better, I believe," said Curtiss, after a pause.

"Something has got to be done," replied the General. "The banking situation in this country at the present moment is simply unendurable; the legitimate banker is practically driven from the field by the speculator. A man finds himself in the position where he has either to submit to the dictation of such men, or else permit himself to be supplanted. It is a new element that has forced itself in. Apparently all a man needs in order to start a bank is credit enough to put up a building with marble columns and bronze gates. I could name you a man who at this moment owns eight banks, and when he started in, three years ago, I don't believe he owned a million dollars."

"But how in the world could he manage it?" gasped Montague.

"Just as I stated," said the General. "You buy a piece of land, with as big a mortgage as you can get, and you put up a million-dollar building and mortgage that. You start a trust company, and you get out imposing advertisements, and promise high rates of interest, and the public comes in. Then you hypothecate your

stock in company number one, and you have your dummy directors lend you more money, and you buy another trust company.
They call that pyramiding—you have heard the term, no doubt,
with regard to stocks; it is a fascinating game to play with banks,
because the more of them you get, the more prominent you
become in the newspapers, and the more the public trusts you."

And the General went on to tell of some of the cases of which
he knew. There was Stewart, the young Lochinvar out of the
West. He had tried to buy the Trust Company of the Republic
long ago, and so the General knew him and his methods. He had
fought the Copper Trust to a standstill in Montana; the Trust
had bought up the Legislature and both political machines, but
Cummings had appealed to the public in a series of sensational
campaigns, and had got his judges into office, and in the end the
Trust had been forced to buy him out. And now he had come to
New York to play this new game of bank-gambling, which paid
even quicker profits than buying courts.—And then there was
Holt, a sporting character, a vulgar man-about-town, who was
identified with everything that was low and vile in the city; he,
too, had turned his millions into banks.—And there was
Cummings, the Ice King, who for years had financed the political machine in the city, and, by securing a monopoly of the
docking-privileges, had forced all his rivals to the wall. He had
set out to monopolize the coastwise steamship trade of the
country, and had bought line after line of vessels by this same
device of "pyramiding"; and now, finding that he needed still
more money to buy out his rivals, he had purchased or started a
dozen or so of trust companies and banks.

"Anyone ought to realize that such things cannot go on indef-
initely," said the General. "I know that the big men realize it. I
was at a directors' meeting the other day, and I heard Waterman
remark that it would have to be ended very soon. Anyone who
knows Waterman would not expect to get a second hint."

"What could he do?" asked Montague.

"Waterman!" exclaimed young Curtiss.

"He would find a way," said the General simply. "That is the
one hope that I see in the situation—the power of a conservative
man like him."

"You trust him, then?" asked Montague.

"Yes," said the General, "I trust him. One has to trust some-body."

"I heard a curious story," put in Harry Curtiss. "My uncle had dinner at the old man's house the other night, and asked him what he thought of the market. 'I can tell you in a sentence,' was the answer. 'For the first time in my life I don't own a security.'"

The General gave an exclamation of surprise. "Did he really say that?" he asked. "Then one can imagine that things will happen before long!"

"And one can imagine why the stock market is weak!" added the other, laughing.

At that moment the door of the dining room was opened, and Mrs. Prentice appeared. "Are you men going to talk business all evening?" she asked. "If so, come into the drawing-room, and talk it to us."

They arose and followed her, and Montague seated himself upon a sofa with Mrs. Prentice and the younger man.

"What were you saying of Dan Waterman?" she asked of the latter.

"Oh, it's a long story," said Curtiss. "You ladies don't care anything about Waterman."

Montague had been watching Lucy out of the corner of his eye, and he could not forbear a slight smile.

"What a wonderful man he is!" said Mrs. Prentice. "I admire him more than any man I know of in Wall Street." Then she turned to Montague. "Have you met him?"

"Yes," said he; and added with a mischievous smile, "I saw him to-day."

"I saw him last Sunday night," said Mrs. Prentice guilelessly. "It was at the Church of the Holy Virgin, where he passes the collection-plate. Isn't it admirable that a man who has as much on his mind as Mr. Waterman has should still save time for the affairs of his Church?"

And Montague looked again at Lucy, and saw that she was biting her lip.

CHAPTER VII

It was a week before Montague saw Lucy again. She came in to lunch with Alice one day, when he happened to be home early.

"I went to dinner at Mrs. Frank Landis's last night," she said. "And who do you think was there—your friend, Mrs. Winnie Duval."

"Indeed," said Montague.

"I had quite a long talk with her," said she. "I liked her very much."

"She is easy to like," he replied. "What did you talk about?"

"Oh, everything in the world but one thing," said Lucy mischievously.

"What do you mean?" asked Montague.

"You, you goose," she answered. "Mrs. Winnie knew that I was your friend, and I had a feeling that every word she was saying was a message to you."

"Well, and what did she have to say to me?" he asked, smiling.

"She wants you to understand that she is cheerful, and not pining away because of you," was the answer. "She told me about all the things that she was interested in."

"Did she tell you about the Babubanana?"

"The what?" exclaimed Lucy.

"Why, when I saw her last," said Montague, "she was turning into a Hindoo, and her talk was all about Swamis, and Gnanis, and so on."

"No, she didn't mention them," said Lucy.

"Well, probably she has given it up, then," said he. "What is it now?"

"She has gone in for anti-vivisection."

"Anti-vivisection!"

"Yes," said the other; "didn't you see in the papers that she had been elected an honorary vice-president of some society or other, and had contributed several thousand dollars?"

"One cannot keep track of Mrs. Winnie in the newspapers," said Montague.

"Well," she continued, "she has heard some dreadful stories about how surgeons maltreat poor cats and dogs, and she would insist on telling me all about it. It was the most shocking dinner-table conversation imaginable."

"She certainly is a magnificent-looking creature," said Lucy, after a pause. "I don't wonder the men fall in love with her. She had her hair done up with some kind of a band across the front, and I declare she might have been an Egyptian princess."

"She has many rôles," said Montague.

"Is it really true," asked the other, "that she paid fifty thousand dollars for a bath-tub?"

"She says she did," he answered. "The newspapers say it, too, so I suppose it is true. I know Duval told me with his own lips that she cost him a million dollars a year; but then that may have been because he was angry."

"Is he so rich as all that?" asked Lucy.

"I don't know how rich he is personally," said Montague. "I know he is one of the most powerful men in New York. They call him the 'System's' banker."

"I have heard Mr. Ryder speak of him," said she.

"Not very favourably, I imagine," said he, with a smile.

"No," said she; "they had some kind of a quarrel. What was the matter?"

"I don't know anything about it," was the answer. "But Ryder is a free lance, and a new man, and Duval works with the big men who don't like to have trespassers about."

Lucy was silent for a minute; her brows were knit in thought. "Is it really true that Mr. Ryder's position is so unstable? I thought the Gotham Trust Company was one of the largest institutions in the country. What are those huge figures that you see in their advertisements—seventy millions—eighty millions—what is it?"

"Something like that," said Montague.

"And is not that true?" she asked.

"Yes, I guess that's true," he said. "I don't know anything about Ryder's affairs, you know—I simply hear the gossip. Everyone says he is playing a bold game. You take my advice, and keep your money somewhere else. You have to be doubly careful because you have enemies."

"Enemies?" asked Lucy, in perplexity.

"Have you forgotten what Waterman said to you?" Montague asked.

"You don't mean to tell me," cried she, "that you think that Waterman would interfere with Mr. Ryder on my account."

"It sounds incredible, I know," said Montague, "but such things have happened before this. If anyone knew the inside stories of the battles that have shaken Wall Street, he would find that many of them had some such beginning."

Montague said this casually, and with nothing in particular in mind. He was not watching his friend closely, and he did not see the effect which his words had produced upon her. He led the conversation into other channels; and he had entirely forgotten the matter the next day, when he received a telephone call from Lucy.

It had been a week since he had written to Smith and Hanson, the lawyers, in regard to the sale of her stock. "Allan," she asked, "no letter from those people yet?"

"Nothing at all," he answered.

"I was talking about it with a friend this morning, and he made a suggestion that I thought was important. Don't you think it might be well to find out whom they are representing?"

"What good would that do?" asked Montague.

"It might help us to get an idea of the prospects," said she. "I fancy they know who wants to sell the stock, and we ought to know who is thinking of buying it. Suppose you write them that you don't care to negotiate with agents."

"But I am in no position to do that," said Montague. "I have already set the people a figure, and they have not replied. We should only weaken our position by writing again. It would be much better to try to interest someone else."

"But I would like to know very much who made that offer," Lucy insisted. "I have heard rumours about the stock, and I really would like to know."

She reiterated this statement several times, and seemed to be very keen about it; Montague wondered a little who had been talking to her, and what she had heard. But warned by what the Major had told him, he did not ask these questions over the 'phone. He answered finally, "I think you are making a mistake, but I will do what you wish."

So he sat down and wrote a note to Messrs. Smith and Hanson, and said that he would like to have a consultation with a member of their firm. He sent this note by messenger, and an hour or so later a wiry little person, with a much-wrinkled face and a shrewd look in his eyes, came into his office and introduced himself as Mr. Hanson.

"I have been talking to my client about the matter of the Northern Mississippi stock," said Montague. "You know, perhaps, that this road was organized under somewhat unusual circumstances; most of the stockholders were personal friends of our family. For this reason my client would prefer not to deal with an agent, if it can possibly be arranged. I wish to find out whether your client would consent to deal directly with the owner of the stock."

Montague finished what he had to say, although while he was speaking he noticed that Mr. Hanson was staring at him with very evident astonishment. Before he had finished, this had changed to a slight sneer.

"What kind of a trick is this you are trying to play on me?" the man demanded.

Montague was too much taken aback to be angry. He simply stared. "I don't understand you," he said.

"You don't, eh?" said the other, laughing in his face. "Well, it seems I know more than you think I do."

"What do you mean?" asked Montague.

"Your client no longer has the stock that you are talking about," said the other.

Montague caught his breath. "No longer has the stock!" he gasped.

"Of course not," said Hanson. "She sold it three days ago." Then, unable to deny himself the satisfaction, he added, "She sold it to Stanley Ryder. And if you want to know any more about it, she sold it for a hundred and sixty thousand dollars, and he gave her a six months' note for a hundred and forty thousand."

Montague was utterly dumfounded. He could do nothing but stare.

It was evident to the other man that his emotion was genuine, and he smiled sarcastically. "Evidently, Mr. Montague," he said, "you have been permitting your client to take advantage of you."

Montague caught himself together, and bowed politely. "I owe you an apology, Mr. Hanson," he said, in a low voice. "I can only assure you that I was entirely helpless in the matter."

Then he rose and bade the man good-morning.

When the door of his office was closed, he caught at the chair by his desk to steady himself, and stood staring in front of him. "To Stanley Ryder!" he gasped.

He turned to the 'phone, and called up his friend.

"Lucy," he said, "is it true that you have sold that stock?"

He heard her give a gasp. "Answer me!" he cried.

"Allan," she began, "you are going to be angry with me——"

"Please answer me!" he cried again. "Have you sold that stock?"

"Yes, Allan," she said, "I didn't mean——"

"I don't care to discuss the matter on the telephone," he said. "I will stop in to see you this afternoon on my way home. Please be in, because it is important." And then he hung up the receiver.

He called at the time he had set, and Lucy was waiting for him. She looked pale, and very much distressed. She sat in a chair, and neither arose to greet him nor spoke to him, but simply gazed into his face.

It was a very sombre face. "This thing has given me a great deal of pain," said Montague; "and I don't want to prolong it any more than necessary. I have thought the matter over, and my mind is made up, so there need be no discussion. It will not be possible for me to have anything further to do with your affairs."

Lucy gave a little gasp: "Oh, Allan!"

He had a valise containing all her papers. "I have brought everything up to date," he said. "There are all the accounts, and the correspondence. Anyone will be able to find exactly how things stand."

"Allan," she said, "this is really cruel."

"I am very sorry," he answered, "but there is nothing else that I can do."

"But did I not have a right to sell that stock to Stanley Ryder?" she cried.

"You had a perfect right to sell it to anyone you pleased," he said. "But you had no right to ask me to take charge of your affairs, and then to keep me in the dark about what you had done."

"But, Allan," she protested, "I only sold it three days ago."

"I know that perfectly well," he said; "but the moment you made up your mind to sell it, it was your business to tell me. That, however, is not the point. You tried to use me as a cat's-paw to pull chestnuts out of the fire for Stanley Ryder."

He saw her wince under the words. "Is it not true?" he demanded. "Was it not he who told you to have me try to get that information?"

"Yes, Allan, of course it was he," said Lucy. "But don't you see my plight? I am not a business woman, and I did not real-ize——"

"You realized that you were not dealing frankly with me," he said. "That is all that I care about, and that is why I am not willing to continue to represent you. Stanley Ryder has bought your stock, and Stanley Ryder will have to be your adviser in the future."

He had not meant to discuss the matter with her any further, but he saw how profoundly he had hurt her, and the old bond between them held him still.

"Can't you understand what you did to me, Lucy?" he exclaimed. "Imagine my position, talking to Mr. Hanson, I knowing nothing and he knowing everything. He knew what you had been paid, and he even knew that you had taken a note."

Lucy stared at Montague with wide-open eyes. "Allan!" she gasped.

"You see what it means," he said. "I told you that you could not keep your doings secret. Now it will only be a matter of a few days before everybody who knows will be whispering that you have permitted Stanley Ryder to do this for you."

There was a long silence. Lucy sat staring before her. Then suddenly she faced Montague.

"Allan!" she cried. "Surely—you understand!"

She burst out violently, "I had a right to sell that stock! Ryder needed it. He is going to organize a syndicate, and develop the property. It was a simple matter of business."

"I have no doubt of it, Lucy," said Montague, in a low voice, "but how will you persuade the world of that? I told you what would happen if you permitted yourself to be intimate with a man like Stanley Ryder. You will find out too late what it means. Certainly that incident with Waterman ought to have opened your eyes to what people are saying."

Lucy gave a start, and gazed at him with horror in her eyes. "Allan!" she panted.

"What is it?" he asked.

"Do you mean to tell me that happened to me because Stanley Ryder is my friend?"

"Of course I do," said he. "Waterman had heard the gossip, and he thought that if Ryder was a rich man, he was a ten-times-richer man."

Montague could see the colour mount swiftly over Lucy's throat and face. She stood twisting her hands nervously together. "Oh, Allan!" she said. "That is monstrous!"

"It is not of my making. It is the way the world is. I found it out myself, and I tried to point it out to you."

"But it is horrible!" she cried. "I will not believe it. I will not yield to such things. I will not be coward enough to give up a friend for such a motive!"

"I know the feeling," said Montague. "I'd stand by you, if it were another man than Stanley Ryder. But I know him better than you, I believe."

"You don't, Allan, you can't!" she protested. "I tell you he is a good man! He is a man nobody understands——"

Montague shrugged his shoulders. "It is possible," he said. "I have heard that before. Many men are better than the things they do in this world; at any rate, they like to persuade themselves that they are. But you have no right to wreck your life out of pity for Ryder. He has made his own reputation, and if he had any real care for you, he would not ask you to sacrifice yourself to it."

"He did not ask me to," said Lucy. "What I have done, I have done of my own free will. I believe in him, and I will not believe the horrible things that you tell me."

"Very well," said Montague, "then you will have to go your own way."

He spoke calmly, though really his heart was wrung with grief. He knew exactly the sort of conversation by which Stanley Ryder had brought Lucy to this state of mind. He could have shattered the beautiful image of himself which Ryder had conjured up; but he could not bear to do it. Perhaps it was an instinct which guided him—he knew that Lucy was in love with the man, and that no facts that anyone could bring would make any difference to her. All he could say was, "You will have to find out for yourself."

And then, with one more look at her pitiful face of misery, he turned and went away, without even touching her hand.

CHAPTER VIII

It was now well on in May, and most of the people of Montague's acquaintance had moved out to their country places; and those who were chained to their desks had yachts or automobiles or private cars, and made the trip into the country every afternoon. Montague was invited to spend another week at Eldridge Devon's, where Alice had been for a week; but he could not spare the time until Saturday afternoon, when he made the trip up the Hudson in Devon's new three-hundred-foot steam-yacht, the *Triton*.

Some unkind person had described Devon to Montague as "a human yawn"; but he appeared to have a very keen interest in life that Saturday afternoon. He had been seized by a sudden conviction that a new and but little advertised automobile had proven its superiority to any of the seventeen cars which he at present maintained in his establishment. He had got three of these new cars, and while Montague sat upon the quarter-deck of the *Triton* and gazed at the magnificent scenery of the river, he had in his ear the monotonous hum of Devon's voice, discussing annular ball-bearings and water-jacketed cylinders.

One of the new cars met them at Devon's private pier, and swept them over the hill to the mansion. The Devon place had never looked more wonderful to Montague than it did just then, with fruit-trees in full blossom, and the wonder of springtime upon everything. For miles about one might see hillsides that were one unbroken stretch of luscious green lawn. But alas, Eldridge Devon had no interest in these hills, except to pursue a golf-ball over them. Montague never felt more keenly the pitiful quality of the people among whom he found himself than when he stood upon the portico of this house—a portico huge enough to belong to some fairy palace in a dream—and gazed at the sweeping vista of the Hudson over the heads of Mrs. Billy Alden and several of her cronies, playing bridge.

After luncheon, he went for a stroll with Alice, and she told him how she had been passing the time. "Young Curtiss was here for a couple of days," she said.

"General Prentice's nephew?" he asked.

"Yes. He told me he had met you," said she. "What do you think of him?"

"He struck me as a sensible chap," said Montague.

"I like him very much," said Alice. "I think we shall be friends. He is interesting to talk to; you know he was in a militia regiment that went to Cuba, and also he's been a cowboy, and all sorts of exciting things. We took a walk the other morning, and he told me some of his adventures. They say he's quite a successful lawyer."

"He is in a very successful firm," said Montague. "And he'd hardly have got there unless he had ability."

"He's a great friend of Laura Hegan's," said Alice. "She was over here to spend the day. She doesn't approve of many people, so that is a compliment."

Montague spoke of a visit which he had paid to Laura Hegan, at one of the neighbouring estates.

"I had quite a talk with her," said Alice. "And she invited me to luncheon, and took me driving. I like her better than I thought I would. Don't you like her, Allan?"

"I couldn't say that I really know her," said Montague. "I thought I might like her, but she did not happen to like me."

"But how could that be?" asked the girl.

Montague smiled. "Tastes are different," he said.

"But there must be some reason," protested Alice. "For she looks at many things in the same way that you do. I told her I thought she would be interested to talk to you."

"What did she say?" asked the other.

"She didn't say anything," answered Alice; and then suddenly she turned to him. "I am sure you must know some reason. I wish you would tell me."

"I don't know anything definite," Montague answered. "I have always imagined it had to do with Mrs. Winnie."

"With Mrs. Winnie!" exclaimed Alice, in perplexing wonder.

"I suppose she heard gossip and believed it," he added.

"But that is a shame!" exclaimed the girl. "Why don't you tell her the truth?"

"*I* tell her?" laughed Montague. "I have no reason for telling her. She doesn't care anything in particular about me."

He was silent for a moment or two. "I thought of it once or twice," he said. "For it made me rather angry at first. I saw myself going up to her, and startling her with the statement, 'What you believe about me is not true!' Then again, I thought I might write her a letter and tell her. But of course it would be absurd; she would never acknowledge that she had believed anything, and she would think I was impertinent."

"I don't believe she would do anything of the sort," Alice answered. "At least, not if she meant what she said to me. She was talking about people one met in Society and how tiresome and conventional it all was. 'No one ever speaks the truth or deals frankly with you,' she said. 'All the men spend their time in paying you compliments about your looks. They think that is all a woman cares about. The more I come to know them, the less I think of them.'"

"That's just it," said Montague. "One cannot feel comfortable knowing a girl in her position. Her father is powerful, and some day she will be enormously rich herself; and the people who gather about her are seeking to make use of her. I was interested in her when I first met her. But when I learned more about the world in which she lives, I shrank from even talking to her."

"But that is rather unfair to her," said Alice. "Suppose all decent people felt that way. And she is really quite easy to know. She told me about some charities she is interested in. She goes down into the slums, on the East Side, and teaches poor children. It seemed to me a wonderfully daring sort of thing, but she laughed when I said so. She says those people are just the same as other people, when you come to know them; you get used to their ways, and then it does not seem so terrible and far off."

"I imagine it would be so," said Montague, with a smile.

"Her father came over to meet her," Alice added. "She said that was the first time he had been out of the city in six months. Just fancy working so hard, and with all the money he has! What in the world do you suppose he wants more for?"

"I don't suppose it is the money," said he. "It's the power. And when you have so much money, you have to work hard to keep other people from taking it away from you."

"He certainly looks as if he ought to be able to protect himself," said the girl. "His face is so grim and forbidding. You would hardly think he could smile, to look at him."

"He is very pleasant, when you know him," said Montague.

"He remembered you, and asked about you," said she. "Wasn't it he who was going to buy Lucy Dupree's stock?"

"I spoke to him about it," he answered, "but nothing came of it."

There was a moment's pause. "Allan," said Alice suddenly, "what is this I hear about Lucy?"

"What do you mean?" he asked.

"People are talking about her and Mr. Ryder. I overheard Mrs. Landis yesterday. It's outrageous!"

Montague did not know what to say. "What can I do?" he asked.

"I don't know," said Alice, "but I think that Victoria Landis is a horrible woman. I know she herself does exactly as she pleases. And she tells such shocking stories——"

Montague said nothing.

"Tell me," asked the other, after a pause, "because you've given up Lucy's business affairs, are we to have nothing to do with her at all?"

"I don't know," he answered. "I don't imagine she will care to see me. I have told her about the mistake she's making, and she chooses to go her own way. So what more can I do?"

That evening Montague found himself settled on a sofa next

to Mrs. Billy Alden. "What's this I hear about your friend, Mrs. Taylor?" she asked.

"I don't know," said he abruptly.

"The fascinating widow seems to be throwing herself away," continued the other.

"What makes you say that?" he asked.

"Vivie Patton told me," said she. "She's an old flame of Stanley Ryder's, you know; and so I imagine it came directly from him."

Montague was dumb; he could think of nothing to say.

"It's too bad," said Mrs. Billy. "She is really a charming creature. And it will hurt her, you know—she is a stranger, and it's a trifle too sudden. Is that the Mississippi way?"

Montague forced himself to say, "Lucy is her own mistress." But his feeble impulse toward conversation was checked by Mrs. Billy's prompt response, "Vivie said she was Stanley Ryder's."

"I understand how you feel," continued the great lady after a pause. "Everybody will be talking about it. Your friend Reggie Mann heard what Vivie said, and he will see to that."

"Reggie Mann is no friend of mine," said Montague, abruptly.

There was a pause. "How in the world do you stand that man?" he asked, by way of changing the conversation.

"Oh, Reggie fills his place," was the reply. And Mrs. Billy gazed about the room. "You see all these women?" she said. "Take them in the morning and put half a dozen of them together in one room; they all hate each other like poison, and there are no men around, and there is nothing to do; and how are you to keep them from quarrelling?"

"Is that Reggie's rôle?" asked the other.

"Precisely. He sees a spark fly, and he jumps up and cracks a joke. It doesn't make any difference what he does—I've known him to crow like a rooster, or stumble over his own feet—anything to raise a laugh."

"Aren't you afraid these epigrams may reach your victim?" asked Montague, with a smile.

"That is what they are intended to do," was the reply.

"I judge you have not many enemies," added Mrs. Billy, after a pause.

"No especial ones," said he.

"Well," said she, "you should cultivate some. Enemies are the spice of life. I mean it, really," she declared, as she saw him smile.

"I had never thought of it," said he.

"Have you ever known what it is to get into a really good fight? You see, you are conventional, and you don't like to acknowledge it. But what is there that wakes one up more than a good, vigorous hatred? Some day you will realize it—the chief zest in life is to go after somebody who hates you, and to get him down and see him squirm."

"But suppose he gets you down?" interposed Montague.

"Ah!" said she, "you mustn't let him! That is what you go into the fight for. Get after him, and do him first."

"It sounds rather barbarous," said he.

"On the contrary," was the answer, "it's the highest reach of civilization. That is what Society is for—the cultivation of the art of hatred. It is the survival of the fittest in a new realm. You study your victim, you find out his weaknesses and his foibles, and you know just where to plant your sting. You learn what he wants, and you take it away from him. You choose your allies carefully, and you surround him and overwhelm him; then when you get through with him, you go after another."

And Mrs. Billy glanced about her at the exquisite assemblage in Mrs. Devon's Louis Seize drawing-room. "What do you suppose these people are here for to-night?" she asked.

CHAPTER IX

A week or two had passed, when one day Oliver called his brother on the 'phone. "Have you or Alice any engagement this evening?" he asked. "I want to bring a friend around to dinner."

"Who is it?" inquired Montague.

"Nobody you have heard of," said Oliver. "But I want you to meet him. You will think he's rather queer, but I will explain to you afterwards. Tell Alice to take my word for him."

Montague delivered the message, and at seven o'clock they went downstairs. In the reception-room they met Oliver and his friend, and it was all that Montague could do to repress a look of consternation.

The name of the personage was Mr. Gamble. He was a little man, a trifle over five feet high, and so fat that one wondered how he could get about alone; his chin and neck were a series of rolls of fat. His face was round like a full moon, and out of it looked two little eyes like those of a pig. It was only after studying them for a while that one discovered that they twinkled shrewdly.

Mr. Gamble was altogether the most vulgar-looking personage that Alice Montague had ever met. He put out a fat little hand to her, and she touched it gingerly, and then gazed at Oliver and his brother in helpless dismay.

"Good-evening. Good-evening," he began volubly. "I am charmed to meet you. Mr. Montague, I have heard so much about you from your brother that I feel as if we were old friends."

There was a moment's pause. "Shall we go into the dining-room?" asked Montague.

He did not much relish the stares which would follow them, but he could see no way out of the difficulty. They went into the room and seated themselves, Montague wondering in a flash whether Mr. Gamble's arms would be long enough to reach to the table in front of him.

"A warm evening," he said, puffing slightly. "I have been on the train all day."

"Mr. Gamble comes from Pittsburg," interposed Oliver.

"Indeed?" said Montague, striving to make conversation. "Are you in business there?"

"No, I am out of business," said Mr. Gamble, with a smile. "Made my pile, so to speak, and got out. I want to see the world a bit before I get too old."

The waiter came to take their orders; in the meantime Montague darted an indignant glance at his brother, who sat and smiled serenely. Then Montague caught Alice's eye, and he could almost hear her saying to him, "What in the world am I going to talk about?"

But it proved not very difficult to talk with the gentleman from Pittsburg. He appeared to know all the gossip of the Metropolis, and he cheerfully supplied the topics of conversation. He had been to Palm Beach and Hot Springs during the winter, and told about what he had seen there; he was going to Newport in the summer, and he talked about the prospects there. If he had the slightest suspicion of the fact that all his conversation was not supremely interesting to Montague and his cousin, he gave no hint of it.

After he had disposed of the elaborate dinner which Oliver ordered, Mr. Gamble proposed that they visit one of the theatres. He had a box all ready, it seemed, and Oliver accepted for Alice before Montague could say a word for her. He spoke for himself, however—he had important work to do, and must be excused.

He went upstairs, and shook off his annoyance and plunged into his work. Some time after midnight, when he had finished, he went out for a breath of fresh air, and as he returned he found Oliver and his friend standing in the lobby of the hotel.

"How do you do, Mr. Montague?" said Gamble. "Glad to see you again."

"Alice has just gone upstairs," said Oliver. "We were going to sit in the café awhile. Will you join us?"

"Yes, do," said Mr. Gamble cordially.

Montague went because he wanted to have a talk with Oliver before he went to bed that night.

"Do you know Dick Ingham?" asked Mr. Gamble, as they seated themselves at a table.

"The Steel man, you mean?" asked Montague. "No, I never met him."

"We were talking about him," said the other. "Poor chap—it really was hard luck, you know. It wasn't his fault. Did you ever hear the true story?"

"No," said Montague, but he knew to what the other referred. Ingham was one of the "Steel crowd," as they were called, and he had been president of the Trust until a scandal had forced his resignation.

"He is an old friend of mine," said Gamble; "he told me all about it. It began in Paris—some newspaper woman tried to blackmail him, and he had her put in jail for three months. And when she got out again, then the papers at home began to get stories about poor Ingham's cutting up. And the public went wild, and they made him resign—just imagine it!"

Gamble chuckled so violently that he was seized by a coughing spell, and had to signal for a glass of water.

"They've got a new scandal on their hands now," said Oliver.

"They're a lively crowd, the Steel fellows," laughed the other. "They want to make Davidson resign, too, but he'll fight them. He knows too much! You should hear his story!"

"I imagine it's not a very savoury one," said Montague, for lack of something to say.

"It's too bad," said the other earnestly. "I have talked to them sometimes, but it don't do any good. I remember Davidson one night: 'Jim,' says he, 'a fellow gets a whole lot of money, and he buys him everything he wants, until at last he buys a woman, and then his trouble begins. If you're buying pictures, there's an end to it—you get your walls covered sooner or later. But you never can satisfy a woman.'" And Mr. Gamble shook his head. "Too bad, too bad," he repeated.

"Were you in the steel business yourself?" asked Montague politely.

"No, no, oil was my line. I've been fighting the Trust, and last year they bought me out, and now I'm seeing the world."

Mr. Gamble relapsed into thought again. "I never went in for that sort of thing myself," he said meditatively; "I am a married man, I am, and one woman is enough for me."

"Is your family in New York?" asked Montague, in an effort to change the subject.

"No, no, they live in Pittsburg," was the answer. "I've got four daughters—all in college. They're stunning girls, I tell you—I'd like you to meet them, Mr. Montague."

"I should be pleased," said Montague, writhing inwardly. But a few minutes later, to his immense relief, Mr. Gamble arose, and bade him good-night.

Montague saw him clamber laboriously into his automobile, and then he turned to his brother.

"Oliver," he asked, "what in the devil does this mean?"

"What mean?" asked Oliver innocently.

"That man," exclaimed the other.

"Why, I thought you would like to meet him," said Oliver; "he is an interesting chap."

"I am in no mood for fooling," said his brother angrily. "Why in the world should you insult Alice by introducing such a man to her?"

"Why, you are talking nonsense!" exclaimed Oliver; "he knows the best people——"

"Where did you meet him?" asked Montague.

"Mrs. Landis introduced him to me first. She met him through a cousin of hers, a naval officer. He has been living in Brooklyn this winter. He knows all the navy people."

"What is it, anyway?" demanded Montague impatiently. "Is it some business affair that you are interested in?"

"No, no," said Oliver, smiling cheerfully—"purely social. He wants to be introduced about, you know."

"Are you going to put him into Society by any chance?" asked the other sarcastically.

"You are warm, as the children say," laughed his brother.

Montague stared at him. "Oliver, you don't mean it," he said. "That fellow in Society!"

"Sure," said Oliver, "if he wants to. Why not?"

"But his wife and his daughters!" exclaimed the other.

"Oh, that's not it—the family stays in Pittsburg. It's only himself this time. All the same," Oliver added, after a pause, "I'd like to wager you that if you were to meet Jim Gamble's four prize daughters, you'd find it hard to tell them from the real thing. They've been to a swell boarding-school, and they've had everything that money can buy them. My God, but I'm tired of hearing about their accomplishments!"

"But do you mean to tell me," the other protested, "that your friends will stand for a man like that?"

"Some of them will. He's got barrels of money, you know. And he understands the situation perfectly—he won't make many mistakes."

"But what in the world does he want?"

"Leave that to him."

"And you," demanded Montague; "you are getting money for this?"

Oliver smiled a long and inscrutable smile. "You don't imagine that I'm in love with him, I trust. I thought you'd be interested to see the game, that's why I introduced him."

"That's all very well," said the other. "But you have no right to inflict such a man upon Alice."

"Oh, stuff!" said Oliver. "She'll meet him at Newport this summer, anyway. How could I introduce him anywhere else, if I wasn't willing to introduce him here? He won't hurt Alice. He gave her a good time this evening, and I wager she'll like him before he gets through. He's really a good-natured chap; the chief trouble with him is that he gets confidential."

Montague relapsed into silence, and Oliver changed the subject. "It seems too bad about Lucy," he said. "Is there nothing we can do about it?"

"Nothing," said the other.

"She is simply ruining herself," said Oliver. "I've been trying to get Reggie Mann to have her introduced to Mrs. Devon, but he says he wouldn't dare to take the risk."

"No, I presume not," said Montague.

"It's a shame," said Oliver. "I thought Mrs. Billy Alden would ask her to Newport this summer, but now I don't believe she'll have a thing to do with her. Lucy will find she knows nobody except Stanley Ryder and his crowd. She has simply thrown herself away."

Montague shrugged his shoulders. "That's Lucy's way," he said.

"I suppose she'll have a good time," added the other. "Ryder is generous, at any rate."

"I hope so," said Montague.

"They say he's making barrels of money," said Oliver; then he added longingly, "My God, I wish I had a trust company to play with!"

"Why a trust company particularly?" asked the other.

"It's the easiest graft that's going," said Oliver. "It's some dodge or other by which they evade the banking laws, and the money comes rolling in in floods. You've noticed their advertisements, I suppose?"

"I have noticed them," said Montague.

"He is adding something over a million a month, I hear."

"It sounds very attractive," said the other; and added dryly, "I suppose Ryder feels as if he owned it all."

"He might just as well own it," was the reply. "If I were going into Wall Street to make money, I'd rather have the control of fifty millions than the absolute ownership of ten."

"By the way," Oliver remarked, after a moment, "the Prentices have asked Alice up to Newport. Alice seems to be quite taken with that young chap, Curtiss."

"He comes round a good deal," said Montague. "He seems a very decent fellow."

"No doubt," said the other. "But he hasn't enough money to take care of a girl like Alice."

"Well," he replied, "that's a question for Alice to consider."

CHAPTER X

One day, a month or so later, Montague, to his great surprise, received a letter from Stanley Ryder.

"Could you make it convenient to call at my office some time this afternoon?" it read. "I wish to talk over with you a business proposition which I believe you will find of great advantage to yourself."

"I suppose he wants to buy my Northern Mississippi stock," he said to himself, as he called up Ryder on the 'phone, and made an appointment.

It was the first time that he had ever been inside the building of the Gotham Trust Company, and he gazed about him at the overwhelming magnificence—huge gates of bronze and walls of exquisite marble. Ryder's own office was elaborate and splendid, and he himself a picture of aristocratic elegance.

He greeted Montague cordially, and talked for a few minutes about the state of the market, and the business situation, in the meantime twirling a pencil in his hand and watching his visitor narrowly. At last he began, "Mr. Montague, I have been for some time working over a plan which I think will interest you."

"I shall be very pleased to hear of it," said Montague.

"Of course, you know," said Ryder, "that I bought from Mrs. Taylor her holdings in the Northern Mississippi Railroad. I bought them because I was of the opinion that the road ought to be developed, and I believed that I could induce someone to take the matter up. I have found the right parties, I think, and the plans are now being worked out."

"Indeed," said the other, with interest.

"The idea, Mr. Montague, is to extend the railroad according to the old plan with which you are familiar. Before we took the matter up, we approached the holders of the remainder of the stock, most of whom, I suppose, are known to you. We made them, through our agents, a proposition to buy their stock at what we considered a fair price; and we have purchased about five thousand shares additional. The prices quoted on the balance were more than we cared to pay, in consideration of the very great cost of the improvements we proposed to undertake. Our idea is now to make a new proposition to these other shareholders. The annual stockholders' meeting takes place next month. At this meeting will be brought up the project for the issue of twenty thousand additional shares, with the understanding that as much of this new stock as is not taken by the present shareholders is to go to us. As I assume that few of them will take their allotments, that will give us control of the road; you can understand, of course, that our syndicate would not undertake the venture unless it could obtain control."

Montague nodded his assent to this.

"At this meeting," said Ryder, "we shall propose a ticket of our own for the new board of directors. We are in hopes that as our proposition will be in the interest of every stockholder, this ticket will be elected. We believe that the road needs a new policy, and a new management entirely; if a majority of the stockholders can be brought to our point of view, we shall take control, and put in a new president."

Ryder paused for a moment, to let this information sink into his auditor's mind; then, fixing his gaze upon him narrowly, he continued: "What I wished to see you about, Mr. Montague, was to make you a proposal to assist us in putting through this project. We should like you, in the first place, to act as our representative, in consultation with our regular attorneys. We should like you to interview privately the stockholders of the road, and explain to them our projects and vouch for our good intentions. If you can see your way to undertake this work for us, we should be glad to place you upon the proposed board of directors; and as soon as we have matters in our hands, we should ask you to become president of the road."

Montague gave an inward start; but practice had taught him to keep from letting his surprise manifest itself very much. He sat for a minute in thought.

"Mr. Ryder," he said, "I am a little surprised at such a proposition from you, seeing that you know so little about me——"

"I know more than you suppose, Mr. Montague," said the other, with a smile. "You may rest assured that I have not broached such a matter to you without making inquiries, and satisfying myself that you were the proper person."

"It is very pleasant to be told that," said Montague. "But I must remind you, also, that I am not a railroad man, and have had no experience whatever in such matters——"

"It is not necessary that you should be a railroad man," was the answer. "One can hire talent of that kind at market prices. What we wish is a man of careful and conservative temper, and, above all, a man of thorough-going honesty: someone who will be capable of winning the confidence of the stockholders, and of keeping it. It seemed to us that you possessed these qualifications. Also, of course, you have the advantage of being familiar with the neighbourhood, and of knowing thoroughly the local conditions."

Montague thought for a while longer. "The offer is a very flattering one," he said, "and I need hardly tell you that it interests me. But before I could properly consider the matter, there is one thing I should have to know—that is, who are the members of this syndicate."

"Why would it be necessary to know that?" asked the other.

"Because I am to lend my reputation to their project, and I should have to know the character of the men that I was dealing with." Montague was gazing straight into the other's eyes.

"You will understand, of course," replied Ryder, "that in a matter of this sort it is necessary to proceed with caution. We cannot afford to talk about what we are going to do. We have enemies who will do what they can to check us at every step."

"Whatever you tell me will, of course, be confidential," said Montague.

"I understand that perfectly well," was the reply. "But I wished first to get some idea of your attitude toward the project—whether or not you would be at liberty to take up this work and to devote yourself to it."

"I can see no reason why I should not," Montague answered.

"It seems to me," said Ryder, "that the proposition can be judged largely upon its own merits. It is a proposition to put through an important public improvement; a road which is in a broken-down and practically bankrupt condition is to be taken up, and thoroughly reorganized, and put upon its feet. It is to have a vigorous and honest administration, a new and adequate equipment, and a new source of traffic. The business of the Mississippi Steel Company, as you doubtless know, is growing with extraordinary rapidity. All this, it seems to me, is a work about the advisability of which there can be no question."

"That is very true," said Montague, "and I will meet the persons who are interested and talk out matters with them; and if their plans are such as I can approve, I should be very glad to join with them, and to do everything in my power to make a success of the enterprise. As you doubtless know, I have five hundred shares of the stock myself, and I should be glad to become a member of the syndicate."

"That is what I had in mind to propose to you," said the other. "I anticipate no difficulty in satisfying you—the project is largely of my own originating, and my own reputation will be behind it. The Gotham Trust Company will lend its credit to the enterprise so far as possible."

Ryder said this with just a trifle of hauteur, and Montague felt that perhaps he had spoken too strenuously. No one could sit in Ryder's office and not be impressed by its atmosphere of magnificence; after all, it was here, and its seventy or eighty million dollars of deposits were real, and this serene and aristocratic gentleman was the master of them. And what reason had Montague for his hesitation, except the gossip of idle and cynical Society people?

Whatever doubts he himself might have, he needed to reflect but a moment to realize that his friends in Mississippi would not share them. If he went back home with the name of Stanley Ryder and the Gotham Trust Company to back him, he would come as a conqueror with tidings of triumph, and all the old friends of the family would rush to follow his suggestions.

Ryder waited awhile, perhaps to let these reflections sink in. Finally he continued: "I presume, Mr. Montague, that you know something about the Mississippi Steel Company. The steel situation is a peculiar one. Prices are kept at an altogether artificial level, and there is room for large profits to competitors of the Trust. But those who go into the business commonly find themselves unexpectedly handicapped. They cannot get the credit they want; orders overwhelm them in floods, but Wall Street will not put up money to help them. They find all kinds of powerful interests arrayed against them; there are raids upon their securities in the market, and mysterious rumours begin to circulate. They find suits brought against them which tend to injure their credit. And sometimes they will find important papers missing, important witnesses sailing for Europe, and so on. Then their most efficient employees will be bought up; their very book-keepers and office-boys will be bribed, and all the secrets of their business passed on to their enemies. They will find that the railroads do not treat them squarely; cars will be slow in coming, and all kinds of petty annoyances will be practised. You know what the rebate is, and you can imagine the part which that plays. In these and a hundred other ways, the path of the independent steel manufacturer is made difficult. And now, Mr. Montague, this is a project to extend a railroad which will be of vast service to the chief competitor of the Steel Trust. I believe that you are man of the world enough to realize that this improvement would have been made long ago, if the Steel Trust had not been able to prevent it. And now the time has come when that project is to be put through in spite of every opposition that the Trust can bring; and I have come to you because I believe that you are a man to be counted on in such a fight."

"I understand you," said Montague quietly; "and you are right in your supposition."

"Very well," said Ryder. "Then I will tell you that the syndicate of which I speak is composed of myself and John S. Price, who has recently acquired control of the Mississippi Steel

Company. You will find out without difficulty what Price's reputation is; he is the one man in the country who has made any real
headway against the Trust. The business of the Mississippi
Company has almost doubled in the past year, and there is no
limit to what it can do, except the size of the plant and the ability of the railroads to handle its product. This new plan would
have been taken up through the Company, but for the fact that
the Company's capital and credit is involved in elaborate extensions. Price has furnished some of the capital personally, and I
have raised the balance; and what we want now is an honest man
to whom we can entrust this most important project, a man who
will take the road in hand and put it on its feet, and make it of
some service in the community. You are the man we have
selected, and if the proposition appeals to you, why, we are
ready to do business with you without delay."

For a minute or two Montague was silent; then he said: "I
appreciate your confidence, Mr. Ryder, and what you say
appeals to me. But the matter is a very important one to me, as
you can readily understand, and so I will ask you to give me until
to-morrow to make up my mind."

"Very well," said Ryder.

Montague's first thought was of General Prentice. "Come to
me any time you need advice," the General had said; so
Montague went down to his office. "Do you know anything
about John S. Price?" he asked.

"I don't know him very well personally," was the reply. "I
know him by reputation. He is a daring Wall Street operator,
and he's been very successful, I am told."

"Price began life as a cowboy, I understand," continued the
General, after a pause. "Then he went in for mines. Ten or fifteen years ago we used to know him as a silver man. Several
years ago there was a report that he had been raiding Mississippi
Steel, and had got control. That was rather startling news, for
everybody knew that the Trust was after it. He seems to have
fought them to a standstill."

"That sounds interesting," said Montague.

"Price was brought up in a rough school," said the General, with a smile. "He has a tongue like a whip-lash. I remember once I attended a creditors' meeting of the American Stove Company, which had got into trouble, and Price started off from the word go. 'Mr. Chairman,' he said, 'when I come into the office of an industrial corporation, and see a stock-ticker behind the president's chair with the carpet worn threadbare in front of it, I know what's the matter with that corporation without asking another word.'

"What do you want to know about him for?" asked the General, after he had finished laughing over this recollection.

"It's a case I'm concerned in," the other answered.

"I tell you who knows about him," said the General. "Harry Curtiss. William E. Davenant has done law business for Price."

"Is that so?" said Montague. "Then probably I shall meet Harry."

"I can tell you a better person yet," said the other, after a moment's thought. "Ask your friend Mrs. Alden; she knows Price intimately, I believe."

So Montague sent up a note to Mrs. Billy, and the reply came, "Come up to dinner. I am not going out." And so, late in the afternoon, he was ensconced in a big leather armchair in Mrs. Billy's private drawing-room, and listening to an account of the owner of the Mississippi Steel Company.

"Johnny Price?" said the great lady. "Yes, I know him. It all depends whether you are going to have him for a friend or an enemy. His mother was Irish, and he is built after her. If he happens to take a fancy to you, he'll die for you; and if you make him hate you, you will hear a greater variety of epithets than you ever supposed the language contained. I first met him in Washington," Mrs. Billy went on reminiscently; "that was fifteen years ago, when my brother was in Congress. I think I told you once how Davy paid forty thousand dollars for the nomination, and went to Congress. It was the year of a Democratic landslide, and they could have elected Reggie Mann if they had felt like it. I went to Washington to live the next winter, and Price was there with a whole army of lobbyists, fighting for free silver. That was

before the craze, you know, when silver was respectable; and
Price was the Silver King. I saw the inside of American government that winter, I can assure you."

"Tell me about it," said Montague.

"The Democratic party had been elected on a low tariff platform," said Mrs. Billy; "and it sold out bag and baggage to the
corporations. Money was as free as water—my brother could
have got his forty thousand back three times over. It was the
Steel crowd that bossed the job, you know—William Roberts
used to come down from Pittsburg every two or three days, and
he had a private telephone wire the rest of the time. I have
always said it was the Steel Trust that clamped the tariff swindle
on the American people, and that's held it there ever since."

"What did Price do with his silver mines?" asked Montague.

"He sold them," said she, "and just in the nick of time. He was
on the inside in the campaign of '96, and I remember one night
he came to dinner at our house and told us that the Republican
party had raised ten or fifteen million dollars to buy the election.
'That's the end of silver,' he said, and he sold out that very
month, and he's been free-lancing it in Wall Street ever since."

"Have you met him yet?" asked Mrs. Billy, after a pause.

"Not yet," he answered.

"He's a character," said she. "I've heard Davy tell about the
first time he struck New York—as a miner, with huge wads of
greenbacks in his pockets. He spent his money like a 'coal-oil
Johnny,' as the phrase is—a hundred-dollar bill for a shine, and
that sort of thing. And he'd go on the wildest debauches; you
can have no idea of it."

"Is he that kind of a man?" said Montague.

"He used to be," said the other. "But one day he had something the matter with him, and he went to a doctor, and the
doctor told him something, I don't know what, and he shut
down like a steel trap. Now he never drinks a drop, and he lives
on one meal a day and a cup of coffee. But he still goes with the
old crowd—I don't believe there is a politician or a sporting-
man in town that Johnny Price does not know. He sits in their
haunts and talks with them until all sorts of hours in the morning, but I can never get him to come to my dinner-parties. 'My

people are human,' he will say; 'yours are sawdust.' Sometime, if you want to see New York, just get Johnny Price to take you about and introduce you to his bookmakers and burglars!"

Montague meditated for a while over his friend's picture. "Somehow or other," he said, "it doesn't sound much like the president of a hundred-million-dollar corporation."

"That's all right," said Mrs. Billy, "but Price will be at his desk bright and early the next morning, and every man in the office will be there, too. And if you think he won't have his wits about him, just you try to fool him on some deal, and see. Let me tell you a little that I know about the fight he has made with the Mississippi Steel Company." And she went on to tell. The upshot of her telling was that Montague borrowed the use of her desk and wrote a note to Stanley Ryder. "From my inquiries about John S. Price, I gather that he makes steel. With the understanding that I am to make a railroad and carry his steel, I have concluded to accept your proposition, subject, of course, to a satisfactory arrangement as to terms."

CHAPTER XI

The next morning Montague had an interview with John S. Price in his Wall Street office, and was retained as counsel in connection with the new reorganization. He accepted the offer, and in the afternoon he called by appointment at the law offices of William E. Davenant.

The first person Montague met there was Harry Curtiss, who greeted him with eagerness. "I was pleased to death when I heard that you were in on this deal," said he; "we shall have some work to do together."

About the table in the consultation-room of Davenant's offices were seated Ryder and Price, and Montague and Curtiss, and, finally, William E. Davenant. Davenant was one of the half-dozen highest-paid corporation lawyers in the Metropolis. He was a tall, lean man, whose clothing hung upon him like rags upon a scare-crow. One of his shoulders was a trifle higher than the other, and his long neck invariably hung forward, so that his thin, nervous face seemed always to be peering about. One had a sense of a pair of keen eyes, behind which a restless brain was constantly plotting. Some people rated Davenant as earning a quarter of a million a year, and it was his boast that no one who made money according to plans which he approved had ever been made to give any of it up.

In curious contrast was the figure of Price, who looked like a well-dressed pugilist. He was verging on stoutness, and his face was round, but underneath the superfluous flesh one could see the jaw of a man of iron will. It was easy to believe that Price had fought his way through life. He spoke sharply and to the point, and he laid bare the subject with a few quick strokes, as of a surgeon's knife.

The first question was as to Montague's errand in the South. There was no need of buying more stock of the road, for if they got the new stock they would have control, and that was all they needed. Montague was to see those holders of the stock whom he knew personally, and to represent to them that he had succeeded in interesting some Northern capitalists in the road, and that they would undertake the improvements on condition that their board of directors should be elected. Price produced a list of the new directors. They consisted of Montague and Curtiss and Ryder and himself; a cousin of the latter's, and two other men, who, as he phrased it, were "accustomed to help me in that way." That left two places to be filled by Montague from among the influential holders of the stock. "That always pleases," said Price succinctly, "and at the same time we shall have an absolute majority."

There was to be voted an issue of a million dollars' worth of bonds, which the Gotham Trust Company would take; also a new issue of twenty thousand shares of stock, which was to be offered *pro rata* to the present stockholders at fifty cents on the dollar. Montague was to state that his clients would take any which these stockholders did not want. He was to use every effort to keep the plan secret, and would make no attempt to obtain the stockholders' list of the road. The reason for this came out a little later, when the subject of the old-time survey was broached.

"I must take steps to get hold of those plans," said Price. "In this, as well as everything else, we proceed upon the assumption that the present administration of the road is crooked."

The next matter to be considered was the charter. "When I get a charter for a railroad," said Price, "I get one that lets me do anything from building a toothpick factory to running flying-machines. But the fools who drew the charter of the Northern Mississippi got permission to build a railroad from Atkin to Opala. So we have to proceed to get an extension. While you are down there, Mr. Montague, you will see the job through with the Legislature."

Upton Sinclair

Montague thought for a moment. "I don't believe that I have much influence with the Legislature," he began.

"That's all right," said Price grimly. "We'll furnish the influence."

Here spoke Davenant. "It seems to me," he said, "that we can just as well arrange this matter without mentioning the Northern Mississippi Railroad at all. If the Steel people get wind of this, we are liable to have all sorts of trouble; the Governor is their man, as you know. The thing to do is to pass a blanket bill, providing that any public-service corporation whose charter ante-dates a certain period may extend its line within certain limits and under certain conditions, and so on. I think that I can draw a bill that will go through before anybody has an idea what it's about."

"Very good," said Price. "Do it that way."

And so they went, from point to point. Price laid down Montague's own course of procedure in a few brief sentences. They had just two weeks before the stockholders' meeting, and it was arranged that he should start for Mississippi upon the following day.

When the conference was over, Montague rode to town with Harry Curtiss.

"What was that Davenant said about the Governor?" he asked, when they were seated in the train.

"Governor Hannis, you mean?" said the other. "I don't know so very much about it, but there's been some agitation down there against the railroads, and Waterman and the Steel crowd put in Governor Hannis to do nothing."

"It was rather staggering to me," said Montague, after a little thought. "I didn't say anything about it, but you know Governor Hannis is an old friend of my father's, and one of the finest men I ever knew."

"Oh yes, I don't doubt that," said Curtiss easily. "They put up these fine, respectable old gentlemen. Of course, he's simply a figurehead—he probably has no idea of what he's really doing. You understand, of course, that Senator Harmon is the real boss of your State."

"I have heard it said," said Montague. "But I never took much stock in such statements——"

"Humph!" said Curtiss. "You'd take it if you'd been in my boots. I used to do business for old Waterman's Southern railroads, and I've had occasion to take messages to Harmon once or twice. New York is the place where you find out about this game!"

"It's not a very pleasant game," said Montague soberly.

"I didn't make the rules," said Curtiss. "You find you either have to play that way or else get out altogether."

The younger man relapsed into silence for a moment, then laughed to himself. "I know how you feel," he said. "I remember when I first came out of college, the twinges I used to have. I had my head full of all the beautiful maxims of the old Professor of Ethics. And they took me on in the legal department of the New York and Hudson Railroad, and we had a case—some kind of a damage suit; and old Henry Corbin—their chief counsel, you know—gave me the papers, and then took out of his desk a typewritten list of the judges of the Supreme Court of the State. 'Some of them are marked with red,' he said; 'you can bring the case before any of them. They are our judges.' Just fancy, you know! And I as innocent as a spring chicken!"

"I should think things like that would get out in the end," said Montague.

Curtiss shrugged his shoulders. "How could you prove it?" he asked.

"But if a certain judge always decided in favour of the railroad——" began Montague.

"Oh, pshaw!" said Curtiss. "Leave that to the judge! Sometimes he'll decide against the railroad, but he'll make some ruling that the higher courts will be sure to upset, and by that time the other fellow will be tired out, and ready to quit. Or else—here's another way. I remember one case that I had that old Corbin told me I'd be sure to win, and I took eleven different exceptions, and the judge decided against me on every single one. I thought I was gone sure—but, by thunder, he instructed the jury in my favour! It took me a long time to see the shrewdness of that; you see, it goes to the higher courts, and they see that the judge has given the losing side every advantage, and has decided purely on the evidence. And of course they haven't the witnesses before them, and don't feel half so well able to judge of the evidence, and so they let the decision stand. There are more ways than one to skin a cat, you see!"

"It doesn't seem to leave much room for justice," said Montague.

To which the other responded, "Oh, hell! If you'd been in this business as long as I have, and seen all the different kinds of shysters that are trying to plunder the railroads, you'd not fret about justice. The way the public has got itself worked up just at present, you can win almost any case you can get before a jury, and there are men who spend all their time hunting up cases and manufacturing evidence."

Montague sat for a while in thought. He muttered, half to himself, "Governor Hannis! It takes my breath away!"

"Get Davenant to tell you about it," said Curtiss, with a laugh. "Maybe it's not so bad as I imagine. Davenant is cynical on the subject of governors, you know. He had an experience a few years ago, when he went up to Albany to try to get the Governor to sign a certain Bill. The Governor went out of his office and left him, and Davenant noticed that a drawer of his desk was open, and he looked in, and there was an envelope with fifty brand-new one-thousand-dollar bills in it! He didn't know what they were there for, but this was a mighty important Bill, and he concluded he'd take a chance. He put the envelope in his pocket; and then the Governor came back, and after some talk about the interests of the public, he told him he'd concluded to veto that Bill. 'Very well,' Mr. Governor,' said the old man, 'I have only this to say,' and he took out the envelope. 'I have here fifty new one-thousand-dollar bills, which are yours if you sign that measure. On the other hand, if you refuse to sign it, I will take the bills to the newspaper men, and tell them what I know about how you got them.' And the Governor turned as white as a sheet, and, by God, he signed the Bill and sent it off to the Legislature while Davenant waited! So you can see why he is sceptical about governors."

"I suppose," said Montague, "that was what Price meant when he said he'd furnish the influence."

"That was what he meant," said the other promptly.

"I don't like the prospect," Montague responded.

The younger man shrugged his shoulders. "What are you going to do about it?" he asked. "Your political machines and your offices are in the hands of pea-nut politicians and grafters who are looking for what's coming to them. If you want anything, you have to pay them for it, just the same as in any other business. You face the same situation every hour—'Pay or quit.'"

"Look," Curtiss went on, after a pause, "take our own case. Here we are, and we want to build a little railroad. It's an important work; it's got to be done. But we might haunt the lobbies of your State Legislature for fifty years, and if we didn't put up, we wouldn't get the charter. And, in the meantime, what do you suppose the Steel Trust would be doing?"

"Have you ever thought what such things will lead to?" asked Montague.

"I don't know," said Curtiss. "I've had a fancy that some day the business men of the country will have to go into politics and run it on business lines."

The other pondered the reply. "That sounds simple," he said. "But doesn't it mean the overthrow of Republican institutions?"

"I am afraid it would," said Curtiss. "But what's to be done?"

There was no answer.

"Do you know any remedy?" he persisted.

"No, I don't know any remedy," said Montague, "but I am looking for one. And I can tell you of this, for a start: I value this Republic more than I do any business I ever got into yet; and if I come to that dilemma, it will be the business that will give way."

Curtiss was watching him narrowly. He put his hand on his shoulder. "That's all right, old man," he said. "But take my advice, and don't let Davenant hear you say that."

"Why not?" asked the other.

The younger man rose from his seat. "Here's my station," he said. "The reason is—it might unsettle his ideas. He's a conservative Democrat, you know, and he likes to make speeches at banquets!"

CHAPTER XII

In spite of his doubts, Montague returned to his old home, and put through the programme as agreed. Just as he had anticipated, he found that he was received as a conquering hero by the holders of the Northern Mississippi stock. He talked with old Mr. Lee, his cousin, and two or three others of his old friends, and he had no difficulty in obtaining their pledges for the new ticket. They were all interested, and eager about the future of the road.

He did not have to concern himself with the new charter. Davenant drew up the Bill, and he wrote that a nephew of Senator Harmon's would be able to put it through without attracting any attention. All that Montague knew was that the Bill passed, and was signed by the Governor.

And then came the day of the stockholders' meeting. He attended it, presenting proxies for the stock of Ryder and Price, and nominated his ticket, greatly to the consternation of Mr. Carter, the president of the road, who had been a lifelong friend of his family's. The new board of directors was elected by the votes of nearly three-fourths of the stock, and the new stock issue was voted by the same majority. As none of the former stockholders cared to take the new stock, Montague subscribed for the whole issue in the name of Ryder and Price and presented a certified check for the necessary deposit.

The news of these events, of course, created great excitement in the neighbourhood; also it did not pass unobserved in New York. Northern Mississippi was quoted for the first time on the "curb," and there was quite a little trading; the stock went up nearly ten points in one day.

Montague received this information in a letter from Harry Curtiss. "You must be prepared to withstand the flatteries of the Steel crowd," he wrote. "They will be after you before long."

Montague judged that he would not mind facing the "Steel crowd"; but he was much troubled by an interview which he had to go through with on the day after the meeting. Old Mr. Carter came to see him, and gave him a feeble hand to shake, and sat and gazed at him with a pitiful look of unhappiness.

"Allan," he said, "I have been president of the Northern Mississippi for fifteen years, and I have served the road faithfully and devotedly. And now—I want you to tell me—what does this mean? Am I——"

Montague could not remember a time when Mr. Carter had not been a visitor at his father's home, and it was painful to see him in his helplessness. But there was nothing that could be done about it; he set his lips together.

"I am very sorry, Mr. Carter," he said; "but I am not at liberty to say a word to you about the plans of my clients."

"Am I to understand, then, that I am to be turned out of my position? I am to have no consideration for all that I have done? Surely——"

"I am very sorry," Montague said again, firmly, "but the circumstances at the present time are such that I must ask you to excuse me from discussing the matter in any way."

A day or two later Montague received a telegram from Price, instructing him to go to Riverton, where the works of the Mississippi Steel Company were located, and to meet Mr. Andrews, the president of the Company. Montague had been to Riverton several times in his youth, and he remembered the huge mills, which were one of the sights of the State. But he was not prepared for the enormous development which had since taken place. The Mississippi Steel Company had now two huge Bessemer converters, in which a volcano of molten flame roared all day and night. It had bought up the whole western side of the town, and cleared away half a hundred ramshackle dwellings; and here were long rows of coke-ovens, and two huge rail-mills, and a plate-mill from which arose sounds like the crashing of the day of doom. Everywhere loomed rows of towering chimneys, and pillars of rolling black smoke. Little miniature railroad tracks ran crisscross about the yards, and engines came puffing and clanking, carrying blazing white ingots which the eye could not bear to face.

Opposite to the entrance of the stockaded yards, the Company had put up a new office building, and upon the top floor of this were the president's rooms.

"Mr. Andrews will be in on the two o'clock train," said his secretary, who was evidently expecting the visitor. "Will you wait in his office?"

"I think I should like to see the works, if you can arrange it for me," said Montague. And so he was provided with a pass and an attendant, and made a tour of the yards.

It was interesting to Montague to see the actual property of the Mississippi Steel Company. Sitting in comfortable offices in Wall Street and exchanging pieces of paper, one had a tendency to lose sight of the fact that he was dealing in material things and disposing of the destinies of living people. But Montague was now to build and operate a railroad—to purchase real cars and handle real iron and steel; and the thought was in his mind that at every step of what he did he wished to keep this reality in mind.

It was a July day, with not a cloud in the sky, and an almost tropical sun blazed down upon the works. The sheds and railroad tracks shimmered in the heat, and it seemed as if the cinders upon which one trod had been newly poured from a fire. In the rooms where the furnaces blazed, Montague could not penetrate at all; he could only stand in the doorway, shading his eyes from the glare. In each of these infernos toiled hundreds of grimy, smoke-stained men, stripped to the waist and streaming with perspiration.

He gazed down the long rows of the blast furnaces, great caverns through the cracks of which the molten steel shone like lightning. Here the men who worked had to have buckets of water poured over them continually, and they drank several gallons of beer each day. He went through the rail-mills, where the flaming white ingots were caught by huge rollers, and tossed about like pancakes, and flattened and squeezed, emerging at the other end in the shape of tortured red snakes of amazing length. At the far end of the mill one could see them laid out in long rows to cool; and as Montague stood and watched them, the thought came to him that these were some of the rails which Wyman had ordered, and which had been the cause of such dismay in the camp of the Steel Trust!

Then he went on to the plate-mill, where giant hammers resounded, and steel plates of several inches thickness were chopped and sliced like pieces of cheese. Here the spectator stared about him in bewilderment and clung to his guide for safety; huge travelling cranes groaned overhead, and infernal engines made deafening clatter upon every side. It was a source of never-ending wonder that men should be able to work in such confusion, with no sense of danger and no consciousness of all the uproar.

Montague's eye roamed from place to place; then suddenly it was arrested by a sight even unusually startling. Across on the other side of the mill was a steel shaft, which turned one of the largest of the rollers. It was high up in the air, and revolving with unimaginable speed, and Montague saw a man with an oil-can in his hand rest the top of a ladder upon this shaft, and proceed to climb up.

He touched his guide upon the arm and pointed. "Isn't that dangerous?" he shouted.

"It's against orders," said the man. "But they will do it."

And even while the words of a reply were upon his lips something happened which turned the sound into a scream of horror. Montague stood with his hand still pointing, his whole body turned to stone. Instantaneously, as if by the act of a magician, the man upon the ladder had disappeared, and instead there was a hazy mist about the shaft, and the ladder tumbling to the ground.

No one else in the mill appeared to have noticed it. Montague's guide leaped forward, dodging a white-hot plate upon its journey to the roller, and rushed down the room to where the engineer was standing by his machinery. For a period which could not have been less than a minute, Montague stood staring at the horrible sight; and then slowly he saw what had been a mist beginning to define itself as the body of a man whirling about the shaft.

Then, as the machinery moved more slowly yet, and the din in the mill subsided, he saw several men raise the ladder again to the shaft and climb up. When the revolving had stopped entirely, they proceeded to cut the body loose; but Montague did not wait to see that. He was white and sick, and he turned and went outside.

He went away to another part of the yards and sat down in the shade of one of the buildings, and told himself that that was the way of life. All the while the din of the mills continued without interruption. A while later he saw four men go past, carrying a stretcher covered with a sheet. It dropped blood at every step, but Montague noticed that the men who passed it gave it no more than a casual glance. When he passed the plate-mill again, he saw that it was busy as ever; and when he went out at the front gate he saw a man, who had been pointed out to him as the foreman of the mill, engaged in picking another labourer from the group which was standing about.

He returned to the president's office and found that Mr. Andrews had just arrived. A breeze was blowing through the office, but Andrews, who was stout, was sitting in his chair with his coat and vest off, vigorously wielding a palm-leaf fan.

"How do you do, Mr. Montague?" he said. "Did you ever know such heat? Sit down—you look done up."

"I have just seen an accident in the mills," said Montague.

"Oh!" said the other. "Too bad. But one finds that steel can't be made without accidents. We had a blast-furnace explosion the other day, and killed eight. They are mostly foreigners, though—'hunkies,' they call them."

Then Andrews pressed a button, summoning his secretary.

"Will you please bring those plans?" he said; and to Montague's surprise he proceeded to spread before him a complete copy of the old reports of the Northern Mississippi survey, together with the surveyor's original drawings.

"Did Mr. Carter let you have them?" Montague asked; and the other smiled a dry smile.

"We have them," he said. "And now the thing for you to do is to have your own surveyors go over the ground. I imagine that when you get their reports, the proposition will look very different."

These were the instructions which came in a letter from Price the next day; and with the help of Andrews, Montague made the necessary arrangements, and the next night he left for New York.

He arrived upon a Friday afternoon. He found that Alice had departed for her visit to the Prentices, and that Oliver was in Newport also. There was an invitation from Mrs. Prentice to him to join them; as Price was away, he concluded that he would treat himself to a rest, and accordingly took an early train on Saturday morning.

Montague's initiation into Society had taken place in the winter-time, and he had yet to witness its vacation activities. When Society's belles and dames had completed a season's round of dinner-parties and dances, they were more or less near to nervous prostration, and Newport was the place which they had selected to retire to and recuperate. It was an old-fashioned New England town, not far from the entrance to Long Island Sound, and from a village with several grocery shops and a tavern, it had been converted by a magic touch of Society into the most famous and expensive resort in the world. Estates had been sold there for as much as a dollar a square foot, and it was nothing uncommon to pay ten thousand a month for a "cottage."

The tradition of vacation and of the country was preserved in such terms as "cottage." You would be invited to a "lawn-party," and you would find a blaze of illumination, and potted plants enough to fill a score of greenhouses, and costumes and jewelled splendour suggesting the Field of the Cloth of Gold. You would be invited to a "picnic" at Gooseberry Point, and when you went there, you would find gorgeous canopies spread overhead, and velvet carpets under foot, and scores of liveried lackeys in attendance, and every luxury one would have expected in a Fifth Avenue mansion. You would take a cab to drive to this "picnic," and it would cost you five dollars; yet you must on no account go without a cab. Even if the destination was just round the corner, a stranger would commit a breach of the proprieties if he were to approach the house on foot.

Coming to Newport, as Montague did, directly from the Mississippi Steel Mills, produced the strangest possible effect upon him. He had seen the social splurge in the Metropolis, and had heard the fabulous prices that people had paid for things. But these thousands and millions had seemed mere abstractions. Now suddenly they had become personified—he had seen where they came from, where all the luxury and splendour were produced! And with every glance that he cast at the magnificence about him, he thought of the men who were toiling in the blinding heat of the blast-furnaces.

Here was the palace of the Wymans, upon the laying out of the grounds of which half a million dollars had been spent; the stone wall which surrounded it was famous upon two continents, because it had cost a hundred thousand dollars. And it was to make steel rails for the Wymans that the slaves of the mills were toiling!

Here was the palace of the Eldridge Devons, with a greenhouse which had cost one hundred and fifty thousand dollars, and which merely supplied the daily needs of its owners. Here was the famous tulip-tree, which had been dug up and brought a distance of fifty miles, at a cost of a thousand dollars. And Montague had seen in the making the steel for one of the great hotels of the Eldridge Devons!

And here was the Walling establishment, the "three-million-dollar palace on a desert," as Mrs. Billy Alden had described it. Montague had read of the famous mantel in its entrance hall, made from Pompeiian marble, and costing seventy-five thousand dollars. And the Wallings were the railroad kings who transported Mississippi steel!

And from that his thoughts roamed on to the slaves of other mills, to the men and women and little children shut up to toil in shops and factories and mines for these people who flaunted their luxury about him. They had come here from every part of the country, with their millions drawn from every kind of labour. Here was the great white marble palace of the Johnsons—the ceilings, floors, and walls of its state apartments had all been made in France; its fences and gates, even its locks and hinges, had been made from special designs by famous artists. The Johnsons were lords of railroads and coal, and ruled the State of West Virginia with a terrible hand. The courts and the Legislature were but branches of old Johnson's office, and Montague knew of mining villages which were owned outright by the Company, and were like stockaded forts; the wretched toilers could not buy so much as a pint of milk outside of the Company store, and even the country doctor could not enter the gates without a pass.

And beyond that was the home of the Warfields, whose fortune came from great department stores, in which young girls worked for two dollars and a half a week, and eked out their existence by prostitution. And this was the summer that Warfield's youngest daughter was launched, and for her debutante dance they built a ballroom which cost thirty thousand dollars—and was torn down the day afterwards!

And beyond this, upon the cliffs, was the castle of the Mayers, whose fortunes came from coal. Montague thought of the young man who had invented the device for the automatic weighing of coal as it was loaded upon steamships. Major Venable had hinted to him that the reason the Coal Trust would not consider it was because they were selling short weight; and since then he had investigated the story, and learned that this was true, and that it was old Mayer himself who had devised the system. And here was his palace, and here were his sons and daughters—among the most haughty and exclusive of Society's entertainers!

So you might drive down the streets and point out the mansions and call the roll of the owners—kings of oil and steel and railroads and mines! Here everything was beauty and splendour. Here were velvet lawns and gardens of rare flowers, and dancing and feasting and merriment. It seemed very far from the sordid strife of commerce, from poverty and toil and death. But Montague carried with him the sight that he had seen in the plate-mill, the misty blur about the whirling shaft, and the shrouded form upon the stretcher, dripping blood.

He was so fortunate as to meet Alice and her friends upon the street, and he drove with them to the bathing beach which Society had purchased and maintained for its own exclusive use. The first person he saw here was Reggie Mann, who came and took possession of Alice. Reggie would not swim himself, because he did not care to exhibit his spindle legs; he was watching with disapproving eye the antics of Harry Percy, his dearest rival. Percy was a man about forty years of age, a cotillion-leader by profession; and he caused keen delight to the spectators upon the beach by wearing a monocle in the water.

They had lunch at the Casino, and then went for a sail in the Prentices' new racing yacht. It was estimated just at this time that there was thirty millions' worth of steam and sailing pleasure-craft in Newport Harbour, and the bay was a wonderful sight that afternoon.

They came back rather early, however, as Alice had an engagement for a drive at six o'clock, and it was necessary for her to change her costume before she went. It was necessary to change it again before dinner, which was at eight o'clock; and Montague learned upon inquiry that it was customary to make five or six such changes during the day. The great ladies of Society were adepts in this art, and prided themselves upon the perfect system which enabled them to accomplish it.

All of Montague's New York acquaintances were here in their splendour: Miss Yvette Simpkins, with her forty trunks of new Paris costumes; Mrs. Billy Alden, who had just launched an aristocratic and exclusive bridge-club for ladies; Mrs. Winnie Duval, who had created a sensation by the rumour of her intention to introduce the simple life at Newport; and Mrs. Vivie Patton, whose husband had committed suicide as the only means of separating her from her Count.

It chanced to be the evening of Mrs. Landis's long-expected dinner-dance. When you went to the Landis mansion, you drove directly into the building, which had a court so large that a coach-and-four could drive around it. The entire ground-floor was occupied by what were said to be the most elaborately equipped stables in the world. Your horses vanished magically through sliding doors at one side, and your carriage at the other side, and in front of you was the entrance to the private apartments, with liveried flunkeys standing in state.

There were five tables at this dinner, each seating ten persons. There was a huge floral umbrella for the centrepiece, and an elaborate colour effect in flowers. During the dance, screens were put up concealing this end of the ballroom, and when they were removed some time after midnight, the tables were found set for the supper, with an entirely new scenic effect.

They danced until broad daylight; Montague was told of parties at which the guests had adjourned in the morning to play tennis. All these people would be up by nine or ten o'clock the next day, and he would see them in the shops and at the bathing beach before noon. And this was Society's idea of "resting" from the labours of the winter season!

After the supper Montague was taken in charge by Mrs. Caroline Smythe, the lady who had once introduced him to her cats and dogs. Mrs. Smythe had become greatly interested in Mrs. Winnie's anti-vivisection crusade, and told him all about it while they strolled out upon the loggia of the Landis palace, and stood and watched the sunrise over the bay.

"Do you see that road back of us?" said Mrs. Smythe. "That is the one the Landises have just succeeded in closing. I suppose you've heard the story."

"No," said Montague, "I haven't heard it."

"It's the joke of Newport," said the lady. "They had to buy up the town council to do it. There was a sight-seers' bus that used to drive up that road every day, and the driver would rein up his horses and stand up and point with his whip.

"'This, ladies and gentlemen,' he'd say, 'is the home of the Landises, and just beyond there is the home of the Joneses. Once upon a time Mr. Smith had a wife and got tired of her, and Mr. Jones had a wife and got tired of her; so they both got divorces and exchanged, and now Mrs. Smith is living in Mr. Jones's house, and Mrs. Jones is living in Mr. Smith's. Giddap!'"

CHAPTER XIII

Alice was up early the next morning to go to church with Harry Curtiss, but Montague, who had really come to rest, was later in rising. Afterwards he took a stroll through the streets, watching the people. He was met by Mrs. de Graffenried, who, after her usual fashion, invited him to come round to lunch. He went, and met about forty other persons who had been invited in the same casual way, including his brother Ollie—and, to his great consternation, Ollie's friend, Mr. Gamble!

Gamble was clad in a spotless yachting costume, which produced a most comical effect upon his expansive person. He greeted Montague with his usual effusiveness. "How do you do, Mr. Montague—how do you do?" he said. "I've been hearing about you since I met you last."

"In what way?" asked Montague.

"I understand that you have gone with the Mississippi Steel Company," said Gamble.

"After a fashion," the other assented.

"You want to be careful—you are dealing with a smooth crowd! Smoother even than the men in the Trust, I fancy." And the little man added, with a twinkle in his eye: "I'm accustomed to say there are two kinds of rascals in the oil business; there are the rascals who found they could rely upon each other, and they are in the Trust; and there are the rascals the devil himself couldn't rely upon, and they're the independents. I ought to know what I'm talking about, because I was an independent myself."

Mr. Gamble chuckled gleefully over this witticism, which was evidently one which he relied upon for the making of conversation. "How do you do, Captain?" he said to a man who was passing. "Mr. Montague, let me introduce my friend Captain Gill."

Montague turned and faced a tall and dignified-looking naval officer. "Captain Henry Gill, of the *Allegheny*."

"How do you do, Mr. Montague?" said the Captain.

"Oliver Montague's brother," added Gamble, by way of further introduction. And then, espying someone else coming whom he knew, he waddled off down the room, leaving Montague in conversation with the officer.

Captain Gill was in command of one of the half-dozen vessels which the Government obligingly sent to assist in maintaining the gaieties of the Newport season. He was an excellent dancer, and a favourite with the ladies, and an old crony of Mrs. de Graffenried's. "Have you known Mr. Gamble long?" he asked, by way of making conversation.

"I met him once before," said Montague. "My brother knows him."

"Ollie seems to be a great favourite of his," said the Captain. "Queer chap."

Montague assented readily.

"I met him in Brooklyn," continued the other, seeming to feel that acquaintance with Gamble called for explanation. "He was quite chummy with the officers at the Navy Yard. Retired millionaires don't often fall in their way."

"I should imagine not," said Montague, smiling. "But I was surprised to meet him here."

"You'd meet him in heaven," said the other, with a laugh, "if he made up his mind that he wanted to go there. He is a good-natured personage; but I can tell you that anyone who thinks that Gamble doesn't know what he's about will make a sad mistake."

Montague thought of this remark at lunch, where he sat at table on the opposite side to Gamble. Next to him sat Vivie Patton, who made the little man the victim of her raillery. It was not particularly delicate wit, but Gamble was tough, and took it all with a cheerful grin.

He was a mystery which Montague could not solve. To be sure he was rich, and spent his money like water; but then there was no scarcity of money in this crowd. Montague found himself wondering whether he was there because Mrs. de Graffenried and her friends liked to have somebody they could snub and wipe their feet upon. His eye ran down the row of people sitting at the table, and the contrast between them and Gamble was an amusing one. Mrs. de Graffenried was fond of the society of young people, and most of her guests were of the second or even the third generation. The man from Pittsburg seemed to be the only one there who had made his own money, and who bore the impress of the money struggle upon him. Montague smiled at the thought. He seemed the very incarnation of the spirit of oil; he was gross and unpleasant, while in the others the oil had been refined to a delicate perfume. Yet somehow he seemed the most human person there. No doubt he was crudely egotistical; and yet, if he was interested in himself, he was also interested in other people, while among Mrs. de Graffenried's intimates it was a sign of vulgarity to be interested in anything.

He seemed to have taken quite a fancy to Montague, for reasons best known to himself. He came up to him again after the luncheon. "This is the first time you've been here, Oliver tells me," said he.

Montague assented, and the other added: "You'd better come and let me show you the town. I have my car here."

Montague had no engagement, and no excuse handy. "It's very good of you——" he began.

"All right," said Gamble. "Come on."

And he took him out and seated him in his huge red touring-car, which had a seat expressly built for its owner, not too deep, and very low, so that his fat little legs would reach the floor.

Gamble settled back in the cushions with a sigh. "Rum sort of place this, ain't it?" said he.

"It's interesting for a short visit," said Montague.

"You can count me out of it," said the other. "I like to spend my summers in a place where I can take my coat off. And I prefer beer to champagne in hot weather, anyhow."

Montague did not reply.

"Such an ungodly lot of snobs a fellow does meet!" remarked his host cheerily. "They have a fine time making fun of me—it amuses them, and I don't mind. Sometimes it does make you mad, though; you feel you'd like to make them swallow you, anyway. But then you think, What's the use of going after something you don't want, just because other people say you can't have it?"

It was on Montague's lips to ask, "Then why do you come here?" But he forbore.

The car sped on down the stately drive, and his companion proceeded to point out the mansions and the people, and to discuss them in his own peculiar style.

"See that yellow brick house in there," said he. "That belongs to Allis, the railroad man. He used to live in Pittsburg, and I remember him thirty years ago, when he had one carriage for his three babies, and pushed them himself, by thunder! He was glad to borrow money from me then, but now he looks the other way when I go by.

"Allis used to be in the steel business six or eight years ago," Gamble continued reminiscently. "Then he sold out—it was the real beginning of the forming of the Steel Trust. Did you ever hear that story?"

"Not that I know of," said Montague.

"Well," said the other, "if you are going to match yourself against the Steel crowd, it's a good idea to know about them. Did you ever meet Jim Stagg?"

"The Wall Street plunger?" asked Montague. "He's a mere name to me."

"His last exploit was to pull off a prize-fight in one of the swell hotels in New York, and one nigger punched the other through a plate-glass mirror. Stagg comes from the wild West, you know, and he's wild as they make 'em—my God, I could tell you some stories about him that'd make your hair stand up! Perhaps you remember some time ago he raided Tennessee Southern in the market and captured it; and old Waterman testified that he took it away from him because he didn't consider he was a fit man to own it. As a matter of fact, that was just pure bluff, for Waterman uses him in little jobs like that all the time. Well, six or eight years ago Stagg owned a big steel plant out West; and there was a mill in Indiana, belonging to Allis, that interfered with their business. One time Stagg and some of his crowd had been on a spree for several days, and late one night they got to talking about Allis. 'Let's buy the —— out,' said Stagg, so they ordered a special and a load of champagne, and away they went to the city in Indiana. They got to Allis's house about four o'clock in the morning, and they rang the bell and banged on the door, and after a while the butler came, half awake.

"'Is Allis in?' asked Stagg, and before the fellow could answer, the whole crowd pushed into the hall, and Stagg stood at the foot of the stairs and roared—he's got a voice like a bull, you know—'Allis, Allis, come down here!'

"Allis came to the head of the stairs in his night-shirt, half frightened to death.

"'Allis, we want to buy your steel plant,' said Stagg.

"'Buy my steel plant!' gasped Allis.

"'Sure, buy it outright! Spot cash! We'll pay you five hundred thousand for it.'

"'But it cost me over twelve hundred thousand,' said Allis.

"'Well, then, we'll pay you twelve hundred thousand,' said Stagg—'God damn you, we'll pay you fifteen hundred thousand!'

"'My plant isn't for sale,' said Allis.

"'We'll pay you two million!' shouted Stagg.

"'It isn't for sale, I tell you.'

"'We'll pay you two million and a half! Come on down here!'

"'Do you mean that?' gasped Allis. He could hardly credit his ears.

"'Come downstairs and I'll write you a cheque!' said Stagg. And so they hauled him down, and they bought his mill. Then they opened some more champagne, and Allis began to get good-natured, too.

"'There's only one thing the matter with my mill,' said he, 'and that's Jones's mill over in Harristown. The railroads give him rebates, and he undersells me.'

"'Well, damn his soul,' said Stagg, 'we'll have his mill, too.'

"And so they bundled into their special again, and about six o'clock in the morning they got to Harristown, and they bought another mill. And that started them, you know. They'd never had such fun in their lives before. It seems that Stagg had just cleaned up ten or twelve millions on a big Wall Street plunge, and they blew in every dollar, buying steel mills—and paying two or three prices for every one, of course."

Gamble paused and chuckled to himself. "What I'm telling you is the story that Stagg told me," said he. "And of course you've got to make allowances. He said he had no idea of what Dan Waterman had been planning, but I fancy that was a lie. Harrison of Pittsburg had been threatening to build a railroad of his own, and take away his business from Waterman's roads, and so there was nothing for Waterman to do but buy him out at three times what his mills were worth. He took the mills that Stagg had bought at the same time. Stagg had paid two or three prices, and Waterman paid him a couple of prices more, and then he passed them on to the American people for a couple of prices more than that."

Gamble paused. "That's where they get these fortunes," he added, waving his fat little hand. "Sometimes it makes a fellow laugh to think of it. Every concern they bought was overcapitalized to begin with; I doubt if two hundred million dollars' worth of honest dollars was ever put into the Steel Trust properties, and they capitalized it at a billion, and now they've raised it to a billion and a half! The men who pulled it off made hundreds of millions, and the poor public that bought the common stock saw it go down to six! They gave old Harrison a four-hundred-million-dollar mortgage on the property, and he sits back and grins, and wonders why a man can't die poor!"

Gamble's car was opposite one of the clubs. Suddenly he signalled his chauffeur to stop.

"Hello, Billy!" he called; and a young naval officer who was walking down the steps turned and came toward him.

"What have you been doing with yourself?" said Gamble. "Mr. Montague, my friend Lieutenant Long, of the Engineers. Where are you going, Billy?"

"Nowhere in particular," said the officer.

"Get in," said Gamble, pointing to the vacant seat between them. "I am showing Mr. Montague the town."

The other climbed in, and they went on. "The Lieutenant has just come up from Brooklyn," he continued. "Lively times we had in Brooklyn, didn't we, Billy? Tell me what you have been doing lately."

"I'm working hard," said the Lieutenant—"studying."

"Studying here in Newport?" laughed Gamble.

"That's easy enough when you belong to the Engineers," said the other. "We are working men, and they don't want us at their balls."

"By the way, Gamble," he added, after a moment, "I was look-ing for you. I want you to help me."

"Me?" said Gamble.

"Yes," said the other. "I have just had notice from the Department that I am one of a board of five that has been appointed to draw up specifications for machine oil for the Navy."

"What can I do about it?" asked Gamble.

"I want you to help me draw them up."

"But I don't know anything about machine oil."

"You cannot possibly know less than I do," said the Lieutenant. "Surely, if you have been in the oil business, you can give me some sort of an idea about machine oil."

Gamble thought for a minute. "I might try," he said. "But would it be the proper thing for me to do? Of course, I'm out of the business myself; but I have friends who might bid for the contract."

"Well, your friends can take their chances with the rest," said the Lieutenant. "I am a friend, too, hang it! And how in the world am I to find out anything about oil?"

Gamble was silent again. "Well, I'll do what I can for you," he said finally. "I'll write out what I know about the qualities of good oil, and you can use it as you think best."

"All right," said the Lieutenant, with relief.

"But you'll have to agree to say nothing about it," said Gamble. "It's a delicate matter, you understand."

"You may trust me for that," said the other, laughing. So the subject was dropped, and they went on with their ride.

Half an hour later Gamble set Montague down at General Prentice's door, and he bade them farewell and went in.

The General was coming down the stairs. "Hello, Allan," he said. "Where have you been?"

"Seeing the place a little," said Montague.

"Come into the drawing-room," said the General. "There's a man in there you ought to know. One of the brainiest newspaper men in Wall Street," he added, as he went across the hall—"the financial man of the *Express*."

Montague entered the room and was introduced to a powerfully built and rather handsome young fellow, who had not so long ago been centre-rush upon a famous football team. "Well, Bates," said the General, "what are you after now?"

"I'm trying to get the inside story of the failure of Grant and Ward," said Bates. "I supposed you'd know about it, if anyone did."

"I know about it," said the General, "but the circumstances are such that I'm not free to tell—at least, not for publication. I'll tell you privately, if you want to know."

"No," said Bates, "I'd rather you didn't do that; I can find it out somehow."

"Did you come all the way to Newport to see me?" asked the General.

"Oh no, not entirely," said Bates. "I'm to get an interview with Wyman about the new bond issue of his road. What do you think of the market, General?"

"Things look bad to me," said Prentice. "It's a good time to reef sail."

Then Bates turned to Montague. "I think I passed you a while ago in the street," he said pleasantly. "You were with James Gamble, weren't you?"

"Yes," said Montague. "Do you know him?"

"Bates knows everybody," put in the General; "that's his specialty."

"I happen to know Gamble particularly well," said Bates. "I

have a brother in his office in Pittsburg. What in the world do you suppose he is doing in Newport?"

"Just seeing the world, so he told me," said Montague. "He has nothing to do since his company sold out."

"Sold out!" echoed Bates. "What do you mean?"

"Why, the Trust has bought him out," said Montague.

The other stared at him. "What makes you think that?" he asked.

"He told me so himself," was the answer.

"Oh!" laughed the other. "Then it's just some dodge that he's up to!"

"You think he hasn't sold?"

"I don't think it, I know it," said Bates. "At any rate, he hadn't sold three days ago. I had a letter from my brother saying that they were expecting to land a big oil contract with the Government that would put them on Easy Street for the next five years!"

Montague said no more. But he did some thinking. Experience had sharpened his wits, and by this time he knew a clue when he met it. A while later, when Bates had gone and his brother had come in with Alice, he got Oliver off in a corner and demanded, "How much are you to get out of that oil contract?"

The other stared at him in consternation. "Good heavens!" he exclaimed. "Did he tell you about it?"

"He told me some things," said Montague, "and I guessed the rest."

Oliver was watching him anxiously. "See here, Allan," he said, "you'll keep quiet about it!"

"I imagine I will," said the other. "It's none of my business, that I can see."

Then suddenly Oliver broke into a smile of amusement. "Say, Allan!" he exclaimed. "He's a clever dog, isn't he!"

"Very clever," admitted the other.

"He's been after that thing for six months, you know—and just as smooth and quiet! It's about the slickest game I ever heard of!"

"But how could he know what officers were to make out those specifications?"

"Oh, that's easy," said the other. "That was the beginning of the whole thing. They got a tip that the contract was to be let, and they had no trouble in finding out the names of the officers. That kind of thing is common, you know; the bureaus in Washington are rotten."

"I see," said Montague.

"Gamble's company is in a bad way," Oliver continued. "The Trust just about had it in a corner. But Gamble saw this chance, and he staked everything on it."

"But what's his idea?" asked the other. "What good will it do him to write the specifications?"

"There are five officers," said Oliver, "and he's been laying siege to every one of them. So now they are all his intimate friends, and every one of them has come to him for help! So there will go into Washington five sets of specifications, all different, but each containing one essential point. You see, Gamble's company has a peculiar kind of oil; it contains some ingredient or other—he told me the name, but I don't remember it now. It doesn't make it any better oil, and it doesn't make it any worse; but it's different from any other oil in the world. And now, don't you see—whatever other requirements are specified, this one quality will surely appear; and there will be only one company in the world that can bid. Of course they will name their own figure, and get a five-year contract."

"I see," said Montague dryly. "It's a beautiful scheme. And how much do you get out of it?"

"He paid me ten thousand at the start," said Oliver; "and I am to get five per cent of the first year's contract, whatever that may be. Gamble says his bid won't be less than half a million, so you see it was worth while!"

And Oliver chuckled to himself. "He's going home to-morrow," he added. "So my job is done. I'll probably never see him again—until his four prize daughters get ready for the market!"

CHAPTER XIV

Montague returned to New York and plunged into his work. The election at which he was scheduled to become president of the Northern Mississippi was not to come off for a month. Meantime there was no lack of work for him to do. It would, of course, be necessary for him to return to Mississippi to live, and he had to close up his affairs in New York. Also he wished to fit himself for the work of superintending a railroad. Through the courtesy of General Prentice, he was introduced to the president of one of the great transcontinental lines, and made a study of that official's office system. He went South again to inspect the work of the surveyors, and to consult with the engineers who had been selected for the work.

Price went ahead with his arrangements to take over the control of the road, without paying any attention to the old management. He sent for Montague one day, and introduced him to a Mr. Haskins, who was to be elected vice-president of the road. Haskins, he said, had formerly been general manager of the Tennessee Southern, and was a practical railroad man. Montague was to rely upon him for all the details of his work.

Haskins was a wiry, nervous little man, with a bad temper and a sarcastic tongue; he worshipped the gospel of efficiency, and in the consultations with him Montague got many curious lights upon the management of railroads. He learned, for instance, that a conspicuous item in the construction account was the money to be used in paying local government boards for right of way through towns and villages. Apparently no one even considered the possibility of securing the privilege by any other methods. Montague did not like the prospect, but he said nothing. Then, again, the road was to purchase its rails and other necessaries from the Mississippi Steel Company, and apparently it was expected to pay a fancy price for these; it was not to ask for any of the discounts which were customary. Also Montague was troubled to learn that the secretary and treasurer of the road were to receive liberal salaries, and that no questions were to be asked, because they were relatives of Price.

All that he put up with; but matters came to a head about ten days before the election, when one day Haskins came to his office with the engineers' estimates, and with his own figures of the probable cost of the extension. Most of the figures were much higher than those which Montague had worked out for himself.

"We ought to do better on those contracts," he said, pointing to some of the items.

"I dare say we might," said Haskins; "but those contracts are to go to the Hill Manufacturing Company."

"I don't understand you," said Montague; "I thought that we were to advertise for bids."

"Yes," replied Haskins, "but that company is to get the contracts, all the same."

"You mean," asked Montague, "that we are not to give them to the lowest bidder?"

"I'm afraid not," said the other.

"Has Price said anything to you to that effect?"

"He has."

"But I don't understand," said Montague; "what is this Hill Manufacturing Company?"

And Haskins smiled. "It's a concern that Price has organized himself," he said.

Montague stared in amazement. "Price himself!" he gasped.

"His nephew is president of the company," added the other.

"Is it a new company?" Montague asked.

"Organized especially for the purpose," smiled the other.

"And what does it manufacture?"

"It doesn't manufacture anything; it simply sells."

"In other words," said Montague, "it's a device whereby Mr.

Price proposes to rob the stockholders of the Northern Mississippi Railroad?"

"You can phrase it that way if you choose," said Haskins quietly; "but I wouldn't advise you to let Price hear you."

"I thank you," responded Montague, and brought the interview to an end.

He took a day to think the matter over. It was not his habit to act upon impulse. He saw that the time had come for him to speak, but he wished to be sure of his course of action before he began. He had dinner at the Club that evening, and, seeing his friend Major Venable ensconced in a big leather chair in the reading-room, he went and sat down beside him.

"How do you do, Major?" he said. "I've got another case that I want to ask you some questions about."

"Always at your service," said the Major.

"It has to do with a railroad," said Montague. "Did you ever hear of such a thing as a railroad president organizing a company to sell supplies to his own road?"

The Major smiled grimly. "Yes, I have heard of it," he said.

"Is it common?" asked Montague.

"Not so common as you might suppose," answered the other. "A railroad president is commonly not an important enough man to be permitted to do it. If it happens to be a big road, and the president is a power in it, why, then he may do it."

"I see," said Montague.

"That was Higgins's trick," said the Major. "Higgins used to go around making speeches to Sunday-schools; he was the kind of man that the newspapers like to refer to as a model citizen and a leader of enterprise. His brothers, and his brothers-in-law, and his cousins, and all his family, went into business in order to sell things to his railroads. I heard of one story—it has never come out, but it's very amusing. Every year the road would advertise its contract for stationery. It used about a million dollars' worth, and there'd be long and most elaborate specifications published—columns and columns. But sandwiched away somewhere in the middle of a paragraph was the provision that the paper must all bear a certain watermark; and that watermark was patented by one of Higgins's companies! It didn't even own so much as a mill—it sublet all the contracts. When Higgins died, he left eighty million dollars; but they juggled the records, and you read in all the newspapers that he left 'a few millions.' That was in Philadelphia, where you can do such things."

Montague sat thinking for a few moments. "But I can't see why they should do it in this case," he said. "The men who are doing it own nearly all of the stock of the road."

"What difference does that make?" asked the Major.

"Why, they are simply plundering their own property," said Montague.

"Tut!" was the reply. "What do they care about the value of the property? They'll unload it before the public finds out; and in the meantime they are probably manipulating the stock. That's the scheme they're working with the street railroads over in Brooklyn, for instance; the more irregular the dividends are, the more violently the stock fluctuates, and the better they like it."

"But this is the case of a railroad that is being built," said Montague; "and they are putting up the money to build it."

"Yes," said the Major, "of course; and then they are paying it back to themselves by this dodge; and they'll still have the stock, and whatever they can get for it will be profit. And if the State Legislature comes along and asks any impertinent questions, they can open their books and say: 'See, we have spent this much for improvements. This is the cost of the road; and if you reduce our freight rates, you will cut off our dividends and confiscate our property.'"

And the Major gazed at Montague with a mischievous twinkle in his eye. "Besides," he said, "another thing. You say they are putting up the money. Are you sure it's their own money? Commonly the greater part of the cost of railroad building is paid by bonds, and they work those bonds off on banks and insurance companies and trust companies. Have you thought of that?"

"No, I hadn't," said Montague.

"I know very few men in Wall Street who use their own money," the Major added. "Take the case of Wyman, for instance. Wyman's railroad keeps a cash surplus of twenty or thirty millions, and Wyman uses that in Wall Street. And when he has made his profit, he takes it and salts it away in village improvement bonds all over the country. Do you see?"

"I see," said Montague. "It's a bad game for the small stockholder."

"It's a bad game for the small man of any sort," said the Major. "When I was young, I can remember, a man would save a little money and put it into an enterprise of some sort, and whatever the profits were, he would get his share of them. But now, you see, the big men have got control, and they are greedier than they used to be. There is nothing hurts them so much as to see the little fellow get any share of the profits, and they've all sorts of schemes for doing him out of it. I could take a week off and tell you about them. You are manufacturing soap, we will say. You find there are too many soap manufacturers and too much soap, and so you propose to combine, and put your rivals out of business, and monopolize the soap market. Your properties are already capitalized at twice what they cost you, because you are naturally hopeful, and that is what you expected they would earn; but now for this new combination you issue stock to the amount of three times this imagined value. Then you fill the Street with rumours of the wonders of your soap combination, and all the privileges and monopolies that you've got, and you unload your stock on the public, we'll say at eighty. You may have sold all your stock, but you've still got control of the corporation. The public is helpless and unorganized, and your men are in. Then the Street begins to hear disturbing rumours about the soap trust, and your board of directors meet and declare that it is impossible to pay any dividends. There is great indignation among the stockholders, and an opposition is organized, but you set the clock an hour ahead, and elect your ticket before the other fellow comes around. Or perhaps the troubles have already knocked the stock down sufficiently low to satisfy you, and you buy a majority of it back. Then the public hears that a new interest has purchased the soap trust, and that a new and honest administration is to be elected; and once more there is hope for soap. You buy a few more plants, and issue more stocks

and bonds, and soap begins to boom, and you sell once more.
You can work that regularly every two or three years, for there
is always a new crop of investors, and nobody but a few people
in Wall Street can possibly keep track of what you are doing."

The Major paused for a while, and sat with a happy smile on
his countenance. "You see," he said, "there are floods and floods
of wealth pouring into Wall Street from all over the country. It
comes to me like a vision. The crops are growing, the mines and
the mills and the factories are working, and here is all the
money. People don't like to take it and hide it up their chimneys—few people have chimneys nowadays. They want to invest
it; and so you prepare investments for them. Take the street
railroads here in New York, for instance. What could be a safer
investment than the street railroads of the Metropolis? An absolute monopoly, and traffic growing so fast that construction can't
keep up with it. Profits are sure. So people buy street railway
stocks and bonds. In this case it's the politicians who organize
the construction companies; that's their share, in return for the
franchises. The insiders have a new scheme—the best yet; it's
like a Gatling gun against bows and arrows. They organize a
syndicate, and get the franchises for nothing, and then sell them
to the company for millions. They've even sold franchises they
didn't own, and railroad lines that hadn't been built. You'll find
some improvements charged for four or five times over, and the
improvements haven't yet been made. First and last they have
paid themselves about thirty million dollars. And, in the meantime, the poor stockholder wonders why he doesn't get his dividends!"

"That's the investment market," the Major continued, after a
pause; "but, of course, the biggest reservoirs of wealth are the
insurance companies and the banks. It's there the real fortunes
are made; you'll find you lose the greater part of your profits,
unless you've got your own banks to take your bonds. I heard an
amusing story the other day of a man who was manufacturing
electrical supplies. He prides himself on being an honest business man, and having nothing to do with Wall Street. His company wanted to extend its business, and it issued a couple of
hundred thousand dollars' worth of bonds, and went to the

Fidelity Insurance Company, and offered them at ninety. 'We
aren't buying any bonds just at present,' said they, 'but suppose
you try the National Trust Company.' So the man went there,
and they offered him eighty for the bonds. That was the best he
could do, and in the end he had to take it. And then the trust
company turns the bonds over to the insurance company at par.
I could name you half a dozen trust companies in New York that
are simply syndicates of insurance people for the working of that
little game."

The Major paused. "You see it?" he asked.

"Yes, I see," Montague replied.

"Is there a trust company by any chance back of this railroad
you are talking of?"

"There is," said Montague; and the Major shrugged his shoulders.

"There you have it," he said. "By-and-by they will find their
first bond issue inadequate to meet the cost of the proposed
improvements. The estimates of the engineers will be found too
low, and there will be another issue of bonds, and your president's company will get another contract. And then the first
thing you know, your president will organize a manufacturing
enterprise along the line of his road, and the road will give him
secret rebates, and practically carry his goods free; or else he'll
organize a private-car line, and make the road pay for the privilege of hauling his cars. Or perhaps he's already got some industrial concern, and is simply building the road as a side-issue."

The Major stopped. He saw that Montague was staring at him
with an expression of perplexity.

"What's the matter?" he asked.

"Good heavens, Major!" exclaimed the other. "Do you know
what road I've been talking about?"

And the Major sank back in his chair and went into a fit of
laughter. He laughed until he was purple in the face, and he
could hardly find breath to speak.

"I really thought you did!" Montague protested. "It's exactly
the situation."

"Oh, dear me!" said the Major, fishing for his pocket-hand-
kerchief to wipe the tears from his eyes. "Dear me! It makes me

think of our district attorney's lemon story. Did you ever hear it?"

"No," said Montague, "I never did."

"It was one of the bright spots in a dreary reform campaign that we had a few years ago. It seems that our young crusader was giving his audience a few illustrations of how dishonest officials could make money in this city.

"'Let us imagine a case,' he said. 'You are an inspector of fruit, and there is a scarcity of lemons in New York. There are two ships full of lemons on the way, and one ship gets in twenty-four hours ahead. Now, the law requires that the fruit be carefully inspected. If you are too careful about it, it will take more than twenty-four hours, and the owner of the cargo will lose a small fortune. So he comes to you and offers you a thousand or two, and you don't stop to open every crate of his lemons.'

"The district attorney told that story at a meeting, and the next morning the newspapers published it. That afternoon he happened to meet a fruit inspector, who was an old friend of his. 'Say, old man,' said the inspector, 'who the devil told you about those lemons?'"

The next morning Montague called at Price's office.

"Mr. Price," he said, "a matter has come up in my discussions with Mr. Haskins about which I thought it necessary to consult you immediately."

"What is it?" asked Price.

"Mr. Haskins informs me that it is understood that the Hill Manufacturing Company is to be favoured in the matter of contracts."

Montague was watching Price narrowly, and he saw his jaw set grimly, and a hostile look come upon his features. Price had been lounging back in his chair; now, slowly, he straightened himself up, as if to receive an attack.

"Well?" he asked.

"Is Mr. Haskins correct?" asked the other.

"He is correct."

"He also stated that you are interested in the company. Is that true?"

"That is true."

"He also stated that the company did not manufacture, but simply sold. Is that true?"

"Yes, that is true."

"Very well, Mr. Price," said Montague. "This is a matter about which we must have an understanding without delay. In my preliminary talks with you I was informed that it was your wish to find a man who should run the road honestly. The situation which you have just outlined to me does not seem to me consistent with that programme."

Montague was prepared for an angry response, but he saw the other make an effort and control himself.

"You must realize, Mr. Montague," he said, "that you are not very familiar with methods in the railroad world. This company of which you speak possesses advantages; it can secure better terms——" Price stopped.

"You mean that it can purchase goods more cheaply than the railroad itself can?" demanded Montague.

"In some cases," began the other.

"Very well, then," he answered. "In any case, where it can obtain better terms, there can be no objection to its receiving the contract. But that does not agree with what Mr. Haskins told me; he gave me to understand that we were to prepare to pay a much higher price, because it would be necessary to give the contracts to the Hill Manufacturing Company; and that was my reason for coming to see you. I wish to have a distinct understanding with you upon this point. While I am president of the Northern Mississippi Railroad, everything that is purchased by the road will be purchased in fair competition, and the concern which will give us the lowest price for the quality of goods we need will receive our order. That is a matter about which there must be left no possible room for misunderstanding. I trust I have made myself clear?"

"You have made yourself clear," said Price; and so the interview terminated.

CHAPTER XV

M ontague went back to his work, but with a heart full of misgivings. He would have liked to persuade himself that that was the end of the episode, but he could not do it. He foresaw that his job as president of a railroad would not be a sinecure.

With all his forebodings, however, he was unprepared for the developments which came the next day. Young Curtiss called him up early in the morning, and asked him to wait at his office. A few minutes later he came in, with evident agitation upon his countenance.

"Montague," he said, "I have something important to tell you. I cannot leave you in ignorance about it. But before I begin, you must understand one thing—that I am taking my future in my hands by telling you. And you must promise me that you will never give the slightest hint that I have spoken to you."

"I will promise," said Montague. "What is it?"

"You must not even let on that you know," added the other. "Price would know that I told you."

"Oh, it's Price!" said Montague. "I'll promise to protect you. What is it?"

"He called up Davenant yesterday afternoon, and told him that you were not to be elected president of the road."

Montague gazed at him in dismay.

"He says you are to be dropped entirely," said the other. "Haskins is to be president. Davenant had to tell me, because I am one of the directors."

"So that's it," Montague whispered to himself.

"Do you know what's the matter?" asked Curtiss.

"Yes, I do," said Montague.

"What is it?"

"It's a long story—just some graft that I wouldn't stand for."

"Oh!" cried Curtiss, with sudden light. "Is it the Hill Manufacturing Company?"

"It is," said Montague.

It was Curtiss's turn to stare in amazement. "My God!" he gasped. "Do you mean that you have thrown up the sponge for that?"

"I haven't thrown up the sponge, by any means," was the answer. "But that's why Price wants to get rid of me."

"But, man!" cried the other. "How perfectly absurd!"

Montague fixed his glance upon him.

"Would you advise me to stand for it?" he asked.

"But, my dear fellow!" said Curtiss. "I've got some stock in that company myself."

Montague sat in silence—he could think of nothing to say after that.

"What in the world do you suppose you have gone into?" protested the other. "A charity enterprise?" Then he stopped, seeing the look of pain upon his friend's face.

He put a hand upon his arm. "See here, old man," he said, "this is too bad, honestly. I understand how you feel, and it's a great credit to you; but you are living in the world, and you have got to be practical. You can't expect to take a railroad and run it as if it were an orphan asylum. You can't expect to do business, if you're going to have notions like that. It's really a shame, to give up a work like this for such a reason."

Montague stiffened. "I assure you I haven't given up yet," he replied grimly.

"But what are you going to do?" protested the other.

"I am going to fight," said he.

"Fight?" echoed Curtiss. "But, man, you are perfectly helpless! Price and Ryder own the road, and they will do as they please with it."

"You are one of the directors of the road," said Montague. "And you know the situation. You know the pledges upon which the election of the new board was secured. Will you vote for Haskins as president?"

"My God, Montague!" protested the other. "What a thing to ask of me! You know perfectly well that I have no power in the road. All the stock I own Price gave me, and what can I do? Why, my whole career would be ruined if I were to oppose him."

"In other words," said Montague, "you are a dummy. You are willing to sell your name and your character for a block of stock. You take a position of trust, and you betray it."

The other's face hardened. "Oh, well," he said, "if that's the way you put it——"

"That's not the way I put it!" said Montague. "That is simply the fact."

"But," cried the other, "don't you realize that they have a majority, even without me?"

"Perhaps they have," said Montague; "but that is no reason why you should not do what is right."

Curtiss arose. "There is nothing more to be said," he remarked. "I am sorry you take it that way. I tried to do you a service."

"I appreciate that," said Montague promptly. "For that I shall always be obliged to you."

"In this fight that you propose to make," said the other, "you must not forget that it is I who have brought you this information——"

"Do not trouble about that," said Montague; "I will protect you. No one shall ever know that I had the information."

Montague spent half an hour pacing up and down his office in thought. Then he called his stenographer, and dictated a letter to his cousin, Mr. Lee, and to each of the three other persons whom he had approached in relation to their votes at the stockholders' meeting. "Certain matters have developed," he wrote, "in connection with the affairs of the Northern Mississippi Railroad, which make me unwilling to accept the position of president. It is also my intention to resign from the board of directors of the road, in which I find myself powerless to prevent the things of which I disapprove."

And then he went on to outline the plan which he intended to carry out, explaining that he offered to those whom he had been the means of influencing the opportunity to go in with him upon equal terms. He requested them to communicate their decisions by telegraph; and two days later he had heard from them all, and was ready for business.

He called up Stanley Ryder, and made an appointment for an interview.

"Mr. Ryder," he said, "a few weeks ago you talked with me in this office, and asked me to assist you in electing your ticket for the Northern Mississippi Railroad. You said that you wished me to become president of the road, and that the reason for the request was that you wanted a man whom you could depend upon for efficient and honest management. I accepted your offer in good faith; and I have made all arrangements, and put in a great deal of hard work at the task of fitting myself for the position. Now I have learned from Mr. Price's own lips that he has organized a company for the purpose of exploiting the road for his own private benefit. I told him that I was unwilling to stand for anything of the sort. Since then I have been thinking the matter over, and I have concluded that this situation will make it impossible for me to co-operate with Mr. Price. I have concluded, therefore, that it would be best for me to resign my position as a member of the board of directors, and also to withdraw my candidacy as president."

Ryder had avoided Montague's gaze; he sat staring in front of him, and tapping nervously with a pencil upon his desk. It was some time before he answered.

"Mr. Montague," he said finally, "I am very sorry indeed to hear your decision. But taking all the circumstances into consideration, it seems to me that perhaps it is a wise one."

Again there was a pause.

"You must permit me to thank you for what you have done," Ryder added. "And I trust that this unfortunate episode will not alter our personal relationship."

"Thank you," said Montague coldly.

He had waited to see what Ryder would say. He waited again, having no mind to help him in his embarrassment.

"As I say," Ryder repeated, "I am very much obliged to you."

"I have no doubt of it," said Montague. "But I trust that you do not expect to end our relationship in any such simple way as that."

He saw Ryder's expression change. "What do you mean?" he asked.

"There is a matter of grave importance which has to be settled before we can part. As you know, I am personally the holder of five hundred shares of Northern Mississippi stock; and to that extent I am interested in the affairs of the road."

"Most certainly," said Ryder quietly, "but I have nothing to do with that. As a stockholder of the road, you look to the board of directors."

"Besides being a stockholder myself," continued Montague, without heeding this remark, "I have also to consider the interests of the three persons whom I interviewed in your behalf. I was the means of inducing these people to vote for the board which you named. I was the means of inducing them to place themselves in the power of Mr. Price and yourself. This being the case, I consider that my honour is involved, and that I am responsible to them."

"What do you expect to do?" asked Ryder.

"I have written to them, informing them of my intention to withdraw. I have not told them the circumstances, but have simply indicated that I find myself powerless to prevent certain things to which I object. I have told them the course I intend to take, and offered them the opportunity to get out upon the same terms as myself. They have accepted the offer, and to-morrow I should receive their stock certificates, and their authorization to dispose of them. I have my own certificates here; and I have to say that I consider you are under obligation to purchase this stock at the same price which you paid for the new stock—namely, fifty dollars a share."

Ryder stared at him. "Mr. Montague, you amaze me!" he said.

"I am sorry for that," said Montague. His voice was hard, and there was a grim look upon his face. He fixed his eyes upon

Ryder. "Nevertheless," he said, "it will be necessary for you to take the stock."

"I am sorry to have to say it," said Ryder, "but this seems to me impertinent."

"The total number of shares," said Montague, "is thirty-five hundred, and the price of them is one hundred and seventy-five thousand dollars."

The two gazed at each other. Ryder saw the look in Montague's eyes, and he did not repeat his sneer.

"May I ask," he inquired, in a low voice, "what reason you have to believe that I will comply with this extraordinary request?"

"I have a very good reason, as I believe you will perceive," said Montague. "You and Mr. Price have purchased this railroad, and you wish to plunder it. That is your privilege—apparently it is the custom here in Wall Street to play tricks upon the investing public. But you cannot play them upon me, because I know too much."

"May I know what you propose to do?" asked Ryder.

"You certainly may," said the other. "I propose to fight. Until you have purchased my stock and the stock of my friends, I shall remain a director in the railroad, and also a candidate for the position of president. I shall make a contest at the next directors' meeting, and if I fail in my purpose there, I shall carry the fight before the public. I flatter myself that my reputation will count for something in my old home; you will not be able to carry matters with quite the same high hand in Mississippi as you are accustomed to in New York. Also, I shall fight you in the courts. I don't happen to know just what is the law in regard to the plundering of a public-service corporation by its own directors, but I shall be very much surprised if I cannot find some ground upon which to put a stop to it. Also, as you know, I am in possession of facts regarding the means whereby you got your new privileges from the State Legislature——"

Ryder was glaring at him in rage. "Mr. Montague," he cried, "this is blackmail!"

"You may call it that if you please," said the other. "I shall not be afraid to face the charge, if you should see fit to bring it in the courts."

Ryder started to reply, then caught his breath and gasped. When he spoke again, he had mastered himself. "It seems to me a most extraordinary thing," he said. "Surely, Mr. Montague, you cannot feel at liberty to make public what you learned from Mr. Price and myself while you were acting as our confidential adviser. Surely you cannot have forgotten the pledge of secrecy which you gave me here in this office!"

"I have not forgotten it," answered Montague. "And I have considered the matter with the greatest care. I consider that it is you who have violated a pledge. I believe that your violation was a deliberate one—that you had intended it from the very beginning. You assured me that you wished an honest administration of the road. I don't believe that you ever did wish it; I believe that you had no thought whatever except to use me as your tool to secure the control of the railroad, without buying out the remaining stockholders. Having accomplished that purpose, you are perfectly willing to have me retire. In fact, I have made up my mind that you never intended that I should be president—I have all along been suspicious about it. But I can assure you that you have struck the wrong man; you cannot play with me in any such manner. I have no idea whatever of retiring from the railroad and permitting you and Mr. Price to exploit it, and to deprive me of the value of my holdings——"

Montague was going on, but the other interrupted him quickly. "I recognize the justice of what you say there, Mr. Montague," said he. "So far as your own shares are concerned, you are entitled to be bought out. I am sure that that is a fair basis——"

"On the contrary," said Montague, "it's a basis the suggestion of which I take as an insult. I have been the means of placing other people at your mercy. My reputation and my promises were used for that purpose, and to whatever I am entitled they are entitled equally. There can be no possible settlement except the one which I have offered you."

Ryder could think of nothing more to say. He sat staring at

the other. And Montague, who had no desire to prolong the interview, arose abruptly.

"I do not expect you to decide this matter immediately," he said. "I presume that you will wish to consult with Mr. Price. I have made known my terms to you, and I have nothing more to say. Either you will accept the terms, or I shall drop everything else, and prepare to fight you at every step. I expect to receive the stock by this evening's mail, and I am obliged to ask you to favour me with a decision by to-morrow noon, so that we can close the matter up without delay."

And with that he bowed formally and took his departure.

The next morning's mail brought him a letter from William E. Davenant.

"MY DEAR MR. MONTAGUE (it read),

"It is reported to me that you have thirty-five hundred shares of the stock of the Northern Mississippi Railroad which you desire to sell at fifty dollars a share. If you will bring the stock to my office to-day, I shall be glad to purchase it."

Having received the letters from the South, Montague went immediately. Davenant was formal; but Montague could catch a humorous twinkle in his eye, which seemed to say, quite confidentially, that he appreciated the joke.

"That ends the matter," he said, as he blotted the last of Montague's signatures. "And I trust you will permit me to say, Mr. Montague, that I consider you an exceedingly capable business man."

"I appreciate the compliment," replied Montague dryly.

CHAPTER XVI

Montague was now a gentleman of leisure, comparatively speaking. He had two cases on his hands, but they did not occupy his time as had the prospect of running a railroad. They were contingency cases, and as they were against large corporations, Montague saw a lean year ahead of him. He smiled bitterly to himself as he realized that the only thing which had given him the courage to break with Price and Ryder had been the money which he and his brother Oliver had won by means of a Wall Street "tip."

He received a letter from Alice. "I am going to remain a couple of weeks longer in Newport," she wrote. "Who do you think has invited me?—Laura Hegan. She has been perfectly lovely to me, and I go to her place next week. You will be interested to know that I had a long talk with her about you; I took occasion to tell her a few things that she ought to know. She was very nice about it. I am hoping that you will come up for another week-end before I leave here. Harry Curtiss is going to spend his vacation here; you might come with him."

Montague smiled to himself as he read this letter. He did not go with Curtiss. But the heat of the city was stifling, and the thought of the surf and the country was alluring, and he went up by way of the Sound one Friday night.

He was invited to dinner at the Hegans'. Jim Hegan was there himself—for the first occasion in three years. Mrs. Hegan declared that it was only because she had gone down to New York and fetched him.

It was the first time that Montague had ever been with Hegan for any length of time. He watched him with interest, for the man was a fascinating problem to him. He was so calm and serene—always courteous and friendly. But what was there behind the mask, Montague wondered. For forty years this man had toiled and fought in the arena of Wall Street, and with only one purpose and one thought in life, so far as Montague knew— the piling up of money. Jim Hegan indulged himself in none of the pleasures of rich men. He had no hobbies, and he seldom went into company. In his busy times it was said that he would use a dozen secretaries, and wear them all out. He was a gigantic engine which drove all day and all night—a machine for the making of money.

Montague did not care much for money himself, and he wondered about it. What did the man want it for? What did he expect to accomplish by it? What was the moral code, the outlook upon life, of a man who gave all his time to heaping up money? What reason did he give to himself for his own career? Some reason he must have, or he could not be so calm and cheerful. Or could it be that he had no thoughts about it at all? Was it simply a blind instinct with him? Was he an animal whose nature it was to make money, and who was untroubled by any scruples? This last idea seemed rather uncanny to Montague; he found himself watching Jim Hegan with a kind of awe; thinking of him as some terrible elemental force, blind and unconscious, like the lightning or the tornado.

For Jim Hegan was one of the wreckers. His fortune had been made by the methods which Major Venable had outlined, by buying aldermen and legislatures and governors; by getting franchises for nothing and selling them for millions; by organizing huge swindles and unloading them upon the public. And here he sat upon the veranda of his home, in the twilight of an August evening, smoking a cigar and telling about an orphan asylum he had founded!

He was cheerful and kindly; he was even benevolent. And could it be that he had no idea of the trail of ruin and distress which he had left behind him? Montague found himself possessed by a sudden desire to penetrate beneath that reserve; to spring at the man and surprise him with some sudden question;

to get at the reality of him, to know him as he was. This air of power and masterfulness, surely that must be the mask that he wore. And how was he to himself? When he was alone with his own conscience? Surely there must come doubt and wonder, unhappiness and loneliness! Surely, then, the lives that he had wrecked must come back to plague him! Surely the memories of treachery and cruelty must make him wince!

And from Hegan, Montague's thoughts went to his daughter. She, too, was serene and stately; Montague wondered what was in her mind. How much did she know about her father's career? Surely she could not have persuaded herself that all that she had heard was calumny. There might be question about this offence or that, but of the great broad facts there could be no question. And did she justify it and excuse it; or was she, too, secretly unhappy? And was this the reason for her pride, and for her bitter speeches? It was a continual topic of chatter in Society, how Laura Hegan had withdrawn herself from all of her mother's affairs, and was interesting herself in work in the slums. Could it be that Nemesis had overtaken Jim Hegan in the form of his daughter? That she was the conscience by which he was to be tormented?

Jim Hegan never talked about his affairs. In all the time that Montague spent with him during his two days at Newport, he gave just one hint for the other to go upon. "Money?" he remarked that evening. "I don't care about money. Money is just chips to me."

Life was a game, and the chips were dollars! What he had played for was power! And suddenly Montague seemed to see the career of this man, unrolled before him like a panorama. He had begun life as an office-boy; and above him were all the heights of business and finance; and the ladder by which to scale them was money. There were rivals with whom he fought; and the overcoming of these rivals had occupied all his time and his thought. If he had bought legislatures, it was because his rivals were trying to buy them. And perhaps then he did not even know that he was a wrecker; perhaps he would not have believed it if anyone had told him! He had travelled all the long journey of his life, trampling out opposition and crushing everything before him, nourishing in his heart the hope that some day, when he had attained to mastery, when there were no more rivals to oppose and thwart him—then he would be free to do good. Then he would no longer have to be a wrecker!

And perhaps that was the meaning of his pitiful little effort— an orphan asylum! It seemed to Montague that the gods must shake with Olympian laughter when they contemplated the spectacle of Jim Hegan and his orphan asylum: Jim Hegan, who could have filled a score of orphan asylums with the children of the men whom he had driven to ruin and suicide!

These thoughts were seething in Montague's mind, and they would not let him rest. Perhaps it was just as well that he did not stay too long that evening. After all, what was the use? Jim Hegan was what circumstances had made him. Vain was the dream of peace and well-doing—there was always another rival! There was a new battle on just at present, if one might believe the gossip of the Street; Hegan and Wyman were at each other's throats. They would fight out their quarrel, and there was no way to prevent them—even though they pulled down the pillars of the nation about each other's heads.

As to just what these men were doing in their struggles, Montague got new information every day. The next morning, while he was sitting on the piazza of one of the hotels watching the people, he recognized a familiar face, and greeted the young engineer, Lieutenant Long, who came and sat down beside him.

"Well," said Montague, "have you heard anything from our friend Gamble?"

"He's back in the bosom of his family again," said the young officer. "He got tired of the splurge."

"Great fellow, Gamble," said Montague.

"I liked him very much," said the Lieutenant. "He's not beautiful to look at, but his heart's in the right place."

Montague thought for a moment, then asked, "Did he ever send you your oil specifications?"

"You bet he did!" said the other. "And say, they were great! The Department will think I'm an expert."

"Indeed," said Montague.

"It was a precious lucky thing for me," said the officer. "I'd have been in quite a predicament, you know."

He paused for a moment. "You cannot imagine," he said, "the position that we naval officers are in. Do you know, I think some word must have got out about that contract."

"You don't say so," said Montague, with interest.

"I do. By Gad, I thought of writing to headquarters about it. I was approached no less than three times!"

"Indeed!"

"Fancy," said the officer. "A young chap got himself introduced to me by one of my friends here. He stuck by me the whole evening, and afterwards, as we were strolling home, he opened up on me in this fashion. He'd heard from a friend in Washington that I was one of those who had been asked to write specifications for the oil contracts of the Navy; and he had some friends who were interested in oil, and who might be able to advise me. He hinted that it might be a good thing for me. Just think of it!"

"I can imagine it was unpleasant."

"I tell you, it sets a man to thinking," said the Lieutenant. "You know the men in our service are exposed to that sort of thing all the time, and some of them are trying to live a good deal higher than their incomes warrant. It's a thing that we've all got to look out for; I can stand graft in politics and in business, but when it comes to the Army and Navy—I tell you, that's where I'm ready to fight."

Montague said nothing. He could think of nothing to say.

"Gamble said something about your being interested in a fight against the Steel Trust," said the other. "Is that so?"

"It was so," replied Montague. "I'm out of it now."

"What we were saying made me think of the Steel Trust," said the Lieutenant. "We get some glimpses of that concern in the Navy, you know."

"I hadn't thought of that," said Montague.

"Ask any man in the service about it," said the Lieutenant. "It's an old scar that we carry round in our souls—it won't heal. I mean the armour-plate frauds."

"Sure enough!" said Montague. He carried a long list of

indictments against the steel kings in his mind; but he had forgotten this one.

"I know about it particularly," the other continued, "because my father was on the board of investigation fifteen years ago. I am disposed to be a little keen on the subject, because what he found out at that time practically caused his death."

Montague darted a keen glance at the young officer, who sat gazing ahead in sombre thought. "Fancy how a naval man feels," he said. "We are told that our ships are going to the Pacific, and any hour the safety of the nation may depend upon them! And they are covered with rotten armour-plate that was made by old Harrison, and sold to the Government for four or five times what it cost. Take one case that I know about—the *Oregon*. I've got a brother on board her to-day. During the Spanish War the whole country was watching her and praying for her. And I could go on board that battleship and put my finger on the spot in her conning-tower that has a series of blow-holes straight through the middle of it—holes that old Harrison had drilled through and plugged up with an iron bar. If ever that plate was struck by a shell, it would splinter like so much glass."

Montague listened, half dazed. "Can one see that?" he cried.

"See it? No!" said the officer. "It's all on the inside of the plate, of course. When they got through with their dirty work, they would treat the surface, and who would ever know the difference?"

"But then, how can *you* know it?" asked Montague.

"I?" said the other. "Because my father had laid before him the history of that plate from the hour it was made until it was put in: the original copies of the doctored shop records, and the affidavits of the man who did the work. He had the same thing in a hundred other cases. I know the man who has the papers at this day."

"You see," continued the Lieutenant, after a pause, "the Government's specifications required that each plate should undergo an elaborate set of treatments; and the shop records of each plate were kept. But, of course, it cost enormous sums to get these treatments right, and even then hundreds of the plates would be bad. So when the shop records came up to the office, young Ingham and Davidson would go over them and edit them and bring them up to standard—that's the way those brilliant young fellows made all the money that they are spending on chorus-girls and actresses to-day. They would have these shop records recopied, but they did not always tear up the old ones, and somebody in the office hid them, and that was how the Government got hold of the story."

"It sounds almost incredible!" exclaimed Montague.

"Take the story of plate H 619, of the *Oregon*," said the Lieutenant. "That was one of a whole group of plates which was selected for the ballistic tests at Indian Head. After it had been selected, it was taken back into the company's shops at night, and secretly retreated three times. And then of course it passed the tests, and the whole group was passed with it!"

"What was done about it?" Montague asked.

"Nothing much was ever done about it," said the other. "The Government could not afford to let the real facts get out. But, of course, the insiders in the Navy knew it, and the memory will last as long as the ships last. As I say, it killed my father."

"But weren't the men punished at all?"

"There was a Board appointed to try the case, and they awarded the Government about six hundred thousand dollars damages. There's a man here in this hotel now who could tell you that story straight from the inside." And the Lieutenant paused and looked about him. Suddenly he stood up, and went to the railing and called to a man who was passing on the other side of the street.

"Hello, Bates," he said; "come here."

"Oh! Bates of the *Express!*" said Montague.

"You know him, do you?" asked the Lieutenant. "Hello, Bates! Have they put you on the Society notes?"

"I'm hunting interviews," replied the other. "How do you do, Mr. Montague? Glad to see you again."

"Come up," said the Lieutenant, "and have a seat."

"I was talking to Mr. Montague about the armour-plate frauds," he added, when the other had drawn up a chair. "I told him you knew the story of the Government's investigation. Bates comes from Pittsburg, you know."

"Yes, I know it," Montague replied.

"That was the first newspaper story I ever worked on," said Bates. "Of course, the Pittsburg papers didn't print the facts, but I got them all the same. And afterwards I came to know intimately a lawyer in Pittsburg who had charge of a secret investigation; and every time I read in the newspapers that old Harrison has given a new library, it sets my blood to boiling all over again."

"I sometimes think," put in the other, "that if somebody could be found to tell that story to the American people, they would rise up and drive the old scoundrel out of the country."

"You could never bring it home to him," said Bates; "he's too cunning for that. He has always turned his dirty work over to other people. You remember during the big strike how he ran away and left the job to William Roberts; and after it was all over, he came back smiling."

"And then buying out the Government to keep himself from being punished!" said the Lieutenant savagely.

Montague turned and looked at him. "What is that?"

"That is the story that Bates's lawyer friend can tell," was the reply. "The Board of officers awarded six hundred thousand dollars' damages to the Government; and the case was appealed to the President of the United States, and he sold out the Navy!"

"Sold it out!" gasped Montague.

The officer shrugged his shoulders. "That's what I call it," he said. "One day old Harrison startled the country by making a speech in support of the President's policy of tariff reform; and the next day the lawyer got word that the award was to be scaled down about seventy-five per cent!"

"And then," added Bates, "William Roberts came down from Pittsburg, and bought up the Democratic party in Congress; and so the country got neither the damages nor the tariff reform. And then a few years later old Harrison sold out to the Steel Trust, and got off with a four-hundred-million-dollar mortgage on the American people!"

Bates sank back in his chair. "It's not a very pleasant topic for a holiday afternoon," he said. "But I can't forget about it. It's this kind of thing that does it, you know—this." And he waved his hand about at the gay assemblage. "The women spending their money on dresses and diamonds, and the men tearing the country to pieces to get it. You'll hear people talk about it—they say these idle rich harm nobody but themselves; but I tell you they spread a trail of corruption wherever they go. Don't you believe that, Mr. Montague?"

"I believe it," said he.

"Take these New England towns," said Bates, "and look at the people in them. The ones who had any energy got up and went West years ago; and those who are left haven't any jaw-bones. Did you ever notice it? And it's just the same, wherever this pleasure crowd comes; it turns the men into boarding-house keepers and lackeys, and the girls into waitresses and prostitutes."

"They learn to take tips!" put in the Lieutenant.

"Everything they've got is for sale to city people," said Bates. "Politically, there isn't a rottener little corner in the whole United States of America than this same Rhode Island—and how much that's saying you can imagine. You can buy votes on election day as you'd buy herrings, and there's not the remotest effort at reform, nor any hope of it."

"You speak bitterly," said Montague.

"I am bitter," said Bates. "But it doesn't often break out. I hold my tongue, and stew in my own juice. We newspaper men see the game, you know. We are behind the scenes, and we see the sawdust put into the dolls. We have to work in this rottenness all the time, and some of us don't like it, I can tell you. But what can we do?"

He shrugged his shoulders. "I spend my time getting facts together, and nine times out of ten my newspaper won't print them."

"I should think you'd quit," said the other, in a low voice.

"What better can I do?" asked the reporter. "I have the facts; and once in a while there comes an explosion, and I get my chance. So I stick at the job. I can't but believe that if you keep putting these things before the people, some time, sooner or later, they will do something. Some time there will come a man who has a conscience and a voice, and who won't sell out. Don't you think so, Mr. Montague?"

"Yes," said Montague, "I think so."

CHAPTER XVII

The summer wore on. At the end of August Alice returned from Newport for a couple of days, having some shopping to do before she joined the Prentices at their camp in the Adirondacks.

Society had here a new way of enjoying itself. People built themselves elaborate palaces in the wilderness, and lived in a fantastic kind of rusticity, with every luxury of civilization included. For this life one needed an entirely separate wardrobe, with doeskin hunting-boots and mountain-climbing skirts—all very picturesque and expensive. It reminded Montague of a jest that he had heard about Mrs. Vivie Patton, whose husband had complained of the expensiveness of her costumes, and requested her to wear simpler dresses. "Very well," she said, "I will get a lot of simple dresses immediately."

Alice spent one evening at home, and she took her cousin into her confidence. "I've an idea, Allan, that Harry Curtiss is going to ask me to marry him. I thought it was right to tell you about it."

"I've had a suspicion of it," said Montague, smiling.

"Harry has a feeling you don't like him," said the girl. "Is that true?"

"No," replied Montague, "not precisely that." He hesitated.

"I don't understand about it," she continued. "Do you think I ought not to marry him?"

Montague studied her face. "Tell me," he said, "have you made up your mind to marry him?"

"No," she answered, "I cannot say that I have."

"If you have," he added, "of course there is no use in my talking about it."

"I wish you would tell me just what happened between you
and him," exclaimed the girl.

"It was simply," said Montague, "that I found that Curtiss was
doing, in a business way, something which I considered improper. Other people are doing it, of course—he has that excuse."

"Well, he has to earn a living," said Alice.

"I know," said the other; "and if he marries, he will have to
earn still more of a living. He will only place himself still tighter
in the grip of these forces of corruption."

"But what did he do?" asked Alice anxiously. Montague told
her the story.

"But, Allan," she said, "I don't see what there is so very bad
about that. Don't Ryder and Price own the railroad?"

"They own some of it," said Montague. "Other people own
some."

"But the other people have to take their chances," protested
the girl; "if they choose to have anything to do with men like
that."

"You are not familiar with business," said the other, "and you
don't appreciate the situation. Curtiss was elected a director—
he accepted a position of trust."

"He simply did it as a favour to Price," said she. "If he hadn't
done it, Price would only have got somebody else. As you say,
Allan, I don't understand much about it, but it seems to me it
isn't fair to blame a young man who has to make his way in the
world, and who simply does what he finds everybody else doing.
Of course, you know best about your own affairs; but it always did
seem to me that you go out of your way to look for scruples."

Montague smiled sadly. "That sounds very much like what he
said, Alice. I guess you have made up your mind to marry him,
after all."

Alice set out, accompanied by Oliver, who was bound for
Bertie Stuyvesant's imitation baronial castle, in another part of
the mountains. Betty Wyman was also to be there, and Oliver
was to spend a full month. But three days later Montague

received a telegram, saying that his brother would arrive in New York shortly after eight that morning, and to wait at his home for him. Montague suspected what this meant; and he had time enough to think it over and make up his mind. "Well?" he said, when Oliver came in. "It's come again, has it?"

"Yes," said Oliver, "it has."

"Another 'sure thing'?"

"Dead sure. Are you coming in?" Oliver asked, after a moment.

Montague shook his head. "No," he said. "I think once was enough for me."

"You don't mean that, Allan!" protested the other.

"I mean it," was the reply.

"But, my dear fellow, that is perfectly insane! I have information straight from the inside—it's as certain as the sunrise!"

"I have no doubt of that," responded Montague. "But I am through with gambling in Wall Street. I've seen enough of it, Oliver, and I'm sick of it. I don't like the emotions it causes in me—I don't like the things it makes me do."

"You found the money came in useful, didn't you?" said Oliver sarcastically.

"Yes, I can use what I've got."

"And when that's gone?"

"I don't know about that yet. But I'll find some way that I like better."

"All right," said Oliver; "it's your own lookout. I will make my own little pile."

They rode down town in a cab together. "Where does your information come from this time?" asked Montague.

"The same source," was the reply.

"And is it transcontinental again?"

"No," said Oliver; "it's another stock."

"What is it?"

"It's Mississippi Steel," was the answer.

Montague turned and stared at him. "Mississippi Steel!" he gasped.

"Why, yes," said Oliver. "What's that to you?" he added, in perplexity.

"Mississippi Steel!" Montague ejaculated again. "Why, didn't you know about my relations with the Northern Mississippi Railroad?"

"Of course," said Oliver; "but what's that got to do with Mississippi Steel?"

"But it's Price who is managing the deal—the man who owns the Mississippi Steel Company!"

"Oh," said the other, "I had forgotten that." Oliver's duties in Society did not give him much time to ask about his brother's affairs.

"Allan," he added quickly, "you won't say anything about it!"

"It's none of my business now," answered the other. "I'm out of it. But naturally I am interested to know. What is it—a raid on the stock?"

"It's going down," said Oliver.

Montague sat staring ahead of him. "It must be the Steel Trust," he whispered, half to himself.

"Nothing more likely," was the reply. "My tip comes from that direction."

"Do you suppose they are going to try to break Price?"

"I don't know; I guess they could do it if they made up their mind to."

"But he owns a majority of the stock!" said Montague. "They can't take it away from him outright."

"Not if he's got it locked up in his safe," was the reply; "and if he's got no debts or obligations. But suppose he's overextended; and suppose some bank has loaned him money on the stock—what then?"

Montague was now keenly interested. He went with his brother while the latter drew his money from the bank, and called at his brokers' and ordered them to sell Mississippi Steel. The other was called away then by an engagement in court, which occupied him for several hours; when he came out, he made for the nearest ticker, and the first figures he saw were Mississippi Steel—quoted at nearly twenty points below the price of the morning!

The bare figures were eloquent to him of many tragedies; they brought before him half a dozen different personalities, with their triumphs and despairs. He could read in them the story of a Titan struggle. Oliver had made his killing; but what of Price and Ryder? Montague knew that most of Price's stock was hypothecated at the Gotham Trust. And now what would become of it? And what would become of the Northern Mississippi?

He bought the afternoon papers. Their columns were full of the sensational events of the day. The bottom had dropped out of Mississippi Steel, as they phrased it. The wildest rumours were afloat. The Company was known to be making enormous extensions, and it was said to have overreached itself; there were whispers that its officers had been speculating, that the Company would be unable to meet the next quarterly payment upon its bonds, that a receivership would be necessary. There were hints that the concern was to be taken over by the Trust, but this was vigorously denied by officers of the latter.

All of which had come like a bolt out of the blue. To Montague it was an amazing and terrible thing. It counted little to him that he was out of the struggle himself; that he no longer had anything to lose personally. He was like a man who had been through an earthquake, and who stood and stared at a gaping crack in the ground. Even though he was safe at the moment, he could not forget that this was the earth upon which he had to spend the rest of his life, and that the next crack might open where he stood.

Montague could not see that there was the least chance for Price and Ryder; he pictured them bowled clean out, and he would not have been surprised to read that they were ruined. But apparently they weathered the storm. The episode passed with no more than a crop of rumours. Mississippi Steel did not go back, however; and he noticed that Northern Mississippi stock had also "gone off" eight or ten points on the curb.

It was a period of great anxiety in the financial world. Men felt the unrest, even though they could not give definite reasons. There had been several panics in the stock market throughout the summer; and leading financiers and railroad presidents seemed to have got the habit of prognosticating the ruin of the country every time they made a speech at a banquet.

But apparently men could not agree about the causes of the trouble. Some insisted that it was owing to the speeches of the President, to his attacks upon the great business interests of the country. Others maintained that the world's supply of capital was inadequate, and pointed out the destruction of great wars and earthquakes and fires. Others argued that there was not enough currency to do the country's business. Now and again there rose above the din the shrill voice of some radical who declared that the stock collapses had been brought about deliberately; but such statements seemed so preposterous that they were received with ridicule whenever they were heeded at all. To Montague the idea that there were men in the country sufficiently powerful to wreck its business, and sufficiently unscrupulous to use their power—the idea seemed to him sensational and absurd.

But he had a talk about it one evening with Major Venable, who laughed at him. The Major named half a dozen men—Waterman and Duval and Wyman among them—who controlled ninety per cent of the banks in the Metropolis. They controlled all three of the big insurance companies, with their resources of four or five hundred million dollars; one of them controlled a great transcontinental railroad system, which alone kept a twenty- or thirty-million dollar "surplus" for stock-gambling purposes.

"If any two or three of those men were to make up their minds," declared the Major, "they could wreck the business of this country in a day. If there were stocks they wanted to pick up, they could knock them to any price they chose."

"How would they do it?" asked the other.

"There are many ways. You noticed that the last big slump began with the worst scarcity of money the Street has known for years. Now, suppose those men should gradually accumulate a lot of cash in the banks, and make an agreement to withdraw it at a certain hour. Suppose that the banks that they own, and the banks where they own directors, and the insurance companies which they control—suppose they all did the same! Can't you imagine the scurrying round for money, the calling in of loans, the rush to realize on holdings? And when you have a public as nervous as ours is, when you have credit stretched to the breaking-point, and everybody involved—don't you see the possibilities?"

"It seems like playing with dynamite," said Montague.

"It's not as bad as it might be," was the answer. "We are saved by the fact that these big men don't get together. There are too many jealousies and quarrels. Waterman wants easy money, and gets the Treasury Department to lend ten millions; Wyman, on the other hand, wants high prices, and he goes into the Street and borrows fifteen millions; and so it goes. There are a half dozen big banking groups in the city——"

"They are still competing, then?" asked Montague.

"Oh yes," said the Major. "For instance, they fight for the patronage of the out-of-town banks. The banks all over the country send their reserves to New York; it's a matter of four or five hundred million dollars, and that's an enormous power. Some of the big banks are agents for one or two thousand institutions, and there's the keenest kind of struggle going on. It's not an easy thing to follow, of course; but they offer all kinds of secret advantages—there's more graft in it than you'd find in Russia."

"I see," said Montague.

"There's only one thing about which the banks are agreed," continued the other. "That is their hatred of the independent trust companies. You see, the national banks have to keep twenty-five per cent reserve, while the trust companies only keep five per cent. Consequently, they do a faster business, and they offer four per cent, and advertise widely, and they are simply driving the banks to the wall. There are over fifty of them in this city alone, and they've got over a billion of the people's money. And, mark my word, that is where you'll see blood spilled before long."

And Montague was destined to remember the prophecy.

A couple of days later occurred an incident which gave him a new light upon the situation. His brother came round one afternoon, with a letter in his hand. "Allan," he said, "what do you make of this?"

Montague glanced at it, and saw that it was from Lucy Dupree.

"MY DEAR OLLIE" (it read),

"I find myself in an embarrassing position, owing to the fact that some business arrangements upon which I had counted have fallen through. The money which I brought with me to New York is nearly all gone, and, as you can understand, my position as a stranger is a difficult one. I have a note which Stanley Ryder gave me for my stock. It is for a hundred and forty thousand dollars, and is due in three months. It occurred to me that you might know someone who has some ready cash, and who would like to purchase the note. I should be very glad to sell it for a hundred and thirty thousand. Please do not mention it except in confidence."

"Now, what in the world do you suppose that means?" said Oliver.

The other stared at him. "I am sure I can't imagine," he replied.

"How much money did Lucy have when she came here?"

"She had three or four thousand dollars. But then, she got ten thousand from Stanley Ryder when he bought that stock."

"She can't have spent any such sum of money!" exclaimed Oliver.

"She may have invested it," said the other thoughtfully.

"Invested nothing!" exclaimed Oliver.

"But that's not what puzzles me," said Montague. "Why doesn't Ryder discount the note himself?"

"That's just it! What business has he letting Lucy hawk his notes about the town?"

"Maybe he doesn't know it. Maybe she's trying to keep her affairs from him."

"Nonsense!" Oliver replied. "I don't believe anything of the sort. What I think is that Stanley Ryder is doing it himself."

"How do you mean?" asked Montague, in perplexity.

"I believe that he is trying to get his own note discounted. I don't believe that Lucy would ever come to us of herself. She'd starve first. She's too proud."

"But Stanley Ryder!" protested Montague. "The President of the Gotham Trust Company!"

"That's all right," said Oliver. "It's his own note, and not the Trust Company's; and I'll wager you he's hard up for cash. There was a big realty company that failed the other day, and I saw that Ryder was one of the stockholders. And he's been hit by that Mississippi Steel slump, and I'll wager you he's scurrying round to raise money. It's just like Lucy, too. Before he gets through, he'll take every dollar she owns."

Montague said nothing for a minute or two. Suddenly he clenched his hands. "I must go up and see her," he said.

Lucy had moved from the expensive hotel to which Oliver had taken her, and rented an apartment on Riverside Drive. Montague went up early the next morning.

She came and stood in the doorway of the drawing-room and looked at him. He saw that she was paler than she had been, and with lines of pain upon her face.

"Allan!" she said. "I thought you would come some day. How could you stay away so long?"

"I didn't think you would care to see me," he said.

She did not answer. She came and sat down, continuing to gaze at him, with a kind of fear in her eyes.

Suddenly he stretched out his hands to her. "Lucy!" he exclaimed. "Won't you come away from here? Won't you come, before it is too late?"

"Where can I go?" she asked.

"Anywhere!" he said. "Go back home."

"I have no home," she answered.

"Go away from Stanley Ryder," said Montague. "He has no right to let you throw yourself away."

"He has not let me, Allan," said Lucy. "You must not blame him—I cannot bear it." She stopped.

"Lucy," he said, after a pause, "I saw that letter you wrote to Oliver."

"I thought so," said she. "I asked him not to. It wasn't fair——"

"Listen!" he said. "Will you tell me what that means? Will you tell me honestly?"

"Yes, I will tell you," she said, in a low voice.

"I will help you if you are in trouble," he continued; "but I will not help Stanley Ryder. If you are permitting him to use you——"

"Allan!" she gasped, in sudden excitement. "You don't think that he knew I wrote?"

"Yes, I thought it," said he.

"Oh, how could you?" she cried.

"I knew that he was in trouble."

"Yes, he is in trouble, and I wanted to help him, if I could. It was a crazy idea, I know; but it was all I could think of."

"Oh, I understand," said Montague.

"And don't you see that I cannot leave him?" exclaimed Lucy. "Now of all times—when he needs help—when his enemies have surrounded him? I'm the only person in the world who cares anything about him—who really understands him——"

Montague could think of nothing to say.

"I know how it hurts you," said Lucy, "and don't think that I have not cared. It is a thought that never leaves me! But some day I know that you will understand; and the rest of the world— I don't care what the world says."

"All right, Lucy," he answered sadly. "I see that I can't be of any help to you. I won't trouble you any more."

CHAPTER XVIII

Another month passed by. Montague was buried in his work, and he caught but faint echoes of the storm that rumbled in the financial world. It was a thing which he thought of with wonder in future times—that he should have had so little idea of what was coming. He seemed to himself like some peasant who digs with bent head in a field, while armies are marshalling for battle all around him; and who is startled suddenly by the crash of conflict, and the bursting of shells about his head.

There came another great convulsion of the stock market. Stewart, the young Lochinvar out of the West, made an attempt to corner copper. One heard wild rumours in relation to the crash which followed. Some said that a traitor had sold out the pool; others, that there had been a quarrel among the conspirators. However that might be, copper broke, and once more there were howling mobs on the curb, and a shudder throughout the financial district. Then suddenly, like a thunderbolt, came tidings that a conference of the big bankers had decreed that the young Lochinvar should be forced out of his New York banks. There were rumours that other banks were involved, and that there were to be more conferences. Then a couple of days later came the news that all the banks of Cummings the Ice King were in trouble, and that he too had been forced from the field.

Montague had never seen anything like the excitement in Wall Street. Everyone he met had a new set of rumours, wilder than the last. It was as if a great rift in the earth had suddenly opened before the eyes of the banking community. But

Montague was at an important crisis in a suit which he had taken up against the Tobacco Trust; and he had no idea that he was in any way concerned in what was taking place. The newspapers were all making desperate efforts to allay the anxiety—they said that all the trouble was over, that Dan Waterman had come to the rescue of the imperilled institutions. And Montague believed what he read, and went his way.

Three or four days after the crisis had developed, he had an engagement to dine with his friend Harvey. Montague was tired after a long day in court, and as no one else was coming, and he did not intend to dress, he walked up town from his office to Harvey's hotel, a place of entertainment much frequented by Society people. Harvey rented an entire floor, and had had it redecorated especially to suit his taste.

"How do you do, Mr. Montague?" said the clerk, when he went to the desk. "Mr. Harvey left a note for you."

Montague opened the envelope, and read a hurried scrawl to the effect that Harvey had just got word that a bank of which he was a director was in trouble, and that he would have to attend a meeting that evening. He had telephoned both to Montague's office and to his hotel, without being able to find him.

Montague turned away. He had no place to go, for his own family was out of town; consequently, he strolled into the dining-room and ate by himself. Afterwards he came out into the lobby, and bought several evening papers, and stood glancing over the headlines.

Suddenly a man strode in at the door, and he looked up. It was Winton Duval, the banker; Montague had never seen him since the time when they had parted in Mrs. Winnie's drawing-room. He did not see Montague, but strode past, his brows knit in thought, and entered one of the elevators.

A moment later Montague heard a voice at his side. "How do you do, Mr. Montague?"

He turned. It was Mr. Lyon, the manager of the hotel, whom Siegfried Harvey had once introduced to him. "Have you come to attend the conference?" said he.

"Conference?" said Montague. "No."

"There's a big meeting of the bankers here to-night,"

remarked the other. "It's not supposed to be known, so don't mention it. How do you do, Mr. Ward?" he added to a man who went past. "That's David Ward."

"Ah," said Montague. Ward was known in the Street by the nickname of Waterman's "office-boy." He was a high-salaried office-boy—Waterman paid him a hundred thousand a year to manage one of the big insurance companies for him.

"So *he's* here, is he?" said Montague.

"Waterman is here himself," said Lyon. "He came in by the side entrance. It's something especially secret, I gather—they've rented eight rooms upstairs, all connecting. Waterman will go in at one end, and Duval at the other, and so the reporters won't know they're together!"

"So that's the way they work it!" said Montague, with a smile.

"I've been looking for some of the newspaper men," Lyon added. "But they don't seem to have caught on."

He strolled away, and Montague stood watching the people in the lobby. He saw Jim Hegan come and enter the elevator, in company with an elderly man whom he recognized as Bascom, the president of the Empire Bank, Waterman's own institution. He saw two other men whom he knew as leading bankers of the System; and then, as he glanced toward the desk, he saw a tall, broad-shouldered man, who had been talking to the clerk, turn around and reveal himself as his friend Bates, of the *Express*.

"Humph!" thought Montague. "The newspaper men are 'on,' after all."

He saw Bates's glance sweep the lobby and rest upon him. Montague made a movement of greeting with his hand, but Bates did not reply. Instead, he strolled towards him, went by without looking at him, and, as he passed, whispered in a low, quick voice, "Please come into the writing-room!"

Montague stood for a moment, wondering; then he followed. Bates went to a corner of the room and seated himself. Montague joined him.

The reporter darted a quick glance about, then began hastily: "Excuse me, Mr. Montague, I didn't want anyone to see us talking. I want to ask you to do me a favour."

"What is it?"

"I'm running down a story. It is something very important. I can't explain it to you now, but I want to get a certain room in this hotel. You have an opportunity to do me the service of a lifetime. I'll explain it to you as soon as we are alone."

"What do you want me to do?" asked Montague.

"I want to rent room four hundred and seven," said Bates. "If I can't get four hundred and seven, I want five hundred and seven, or six hundred and seven. I daren't ask for it myself, because the clerk knows me. But he'll let you have it."

"But how shall I ask for it?" said Montague.

"Just ask," said Bates; "it will be all right."

Montague looked at him. He could see that his friend was labouring under great excitement.

"Please! please!" he whispered, putting his hand on Montague's arm. And Montague said, "All right."

He got up and strolled into the lobby again, and went to the desk.

"Good evening, Mr. Montague," said the clerk. "Mr. Harvey hasn't returned."

"I know it," said Montague. "I would like to get a room for the evening. I would like to be near a friend. Could I get a room on the fourth floor?"

"Fourth?" said the clerk, and turned to look at his schedule on the wall. "Whereabouts—front or back?"

"Have you four hundred and five?" asked Montague.

"Four hundred and five? No, that's rented. We have four hundred and one—four hundred and six, on the other side of the hall—four hundred and seven——"

"I'll take four hundred and seven," said Montague.

"Four dollars a day," said the clerk, as he took down the key.

Not having any baggage, Montague paid in advance, and followed the boy to the elevator. Bates followed him, and another man, a little wiry chap, carrying a dress-suit case, also entered with them, and got out at the fourth floor.

The boy opened the door, and the three men entered the room. The boy turned on the light, and proceeded to lower the shades and the windows, and to do enough fixing to earn his tip.

Then he went out, closing the door behind him; and Bates sank upon the bed and put his hands to his forehead and gasped, "Oh, my God!"

The young man who accompanied him had set down his suit-case, and he now sat down on one of the chairs, and proceeded to lean back and laugh hilariously.

Montague stood staring from one to the other.

"My God, my God!" said Bates again. "I hope I may never go through with a job like this—I believe my hair will be grey before morning!"

"You forget that you haven't told me yet what's the matter," said Montague.

"Sure enough," said Bates.

And suddenly he sat up and stared at him.

"Mr. Montague," he exclaimed, "don't go back on us! You've no idea how I've been working—and it will be the biggest scoop of a lifetime. Promise me that you won't give us away!"

"I cannot promise you," said Montague, laughing in spite of himself, "until you tell me what it is."

"I'm afraid you are not going to like it," said Bates. "It was a mean trick to play on you, but I was desperate. I didn't dare take the risk myself, and Rodney wasn't dressed for the occasion."

"You haven't introduced your friend," said Montague.

"Oh, excuse me," said Bates. "Mr. Rodney, one of our office-men."

"And now tell me about it," said Montague, taking a seat.

"It's the conference," said Bates. "We got a tip about it an hour or so ago. They meet in the room underneath us."

"What of it?" asked Montague.

"We want to find out what's going on," said Bates.

"But how?"

"Through the window. We've got a rope here." And Bates pointed toward the suit-case.

Montague stared at him, dumfounded. "A rope!" he gasped. "You are going to let him down from the window?"

"Sure thing," said Bates; "it's a rear window, and quite safe."

"But, for Heaven's sake, man!" gasped the other, "suppose the rope breaks?"

"Oh, it won't break," was the reply; "we've got the right sort of rope."

"But how will you ever get him up again?" Montague exclaimed.

"That's all right," said Bates; "he can climb up, or else we can let him down to the ground. We've got rope enough."

"But suppose he loses his grip! Suppose——"

"That's all right," said Bates easily. "You leave that to Rodney. He's nimble—he began life as a steeple-jack. That's why I picked him."

Rodney grinned. "I'll take my chances," he said.

Montague gazed from one to the other, unable to think of another word to say.

"Tell me, Mr. Bates," he asked finally, "do you often do this in your profession?"

"I've done it once before," was the reply. "I wanted some photographs in a murder case. I've often tried back windows, and fire-escapes, and such things. I used to be a police reporter, you know, and I learned bad habits."

"But," said Montague, "suppose you were caught?"

"Oh, pshaw!" said he. "The office would soon fix that up. The police never bother a newspaper man."

There was a pause. "Mr. Montague," said Bates earnestly, "I know this is a tough proposition—but think what it means. We get word about this conference. Waterman is here—and Duval—think of that! Dan Waterman and the Oil Trust getting together! The managing editor sent for me himself, and he said, 'Bates, get that story.' And what am I to do? There's about as much chance of my finding out what goes on in that conference——"

He stopped. "Think of what it may mean, Mr. Montague," he cried. "They will decide on to-morrow's moves! It may turn the stock market upside down. Think of what you could do with the information!"

"No," said Montague, shaking his head; "don't go at me that way."

Bates was gazing at him. "I beg your pardon," he said; "but, then, maybe you have interests of your own; or your friends—surely this situation——"

"No, not that either," said Montague, smiling; and Bates broke into a laugh.

"Well, then," he said, "just for the sport of it! Just to fool them!"

"That's more like it," said Montague.

"Of course, it's your room," said Bates. "You can stop us, if you insist. But you needn't stay if you don't want to. We'll take all the risk; and you may be sure that if we were caught, the hotel would suppress it. You can trust me to clear your name——"

"I'll stay," said Montague. "I'll see it through."

Bates jumped up and stretched out his hand. "Good!" he cried. "Put it there!"

In the meantime, Rodney pounced upon the dress-suit case, and opened it, taking out a coil of wire rope, very light and flexible, and a short piece of board. He proceeded to make a loop with the rope, and in this he fixed the board for a seat. He then took the blankets from the bed and folded them. He took out a pair of heavy calfskin gloves, which he tossed to Bates, and a ball of twine, one end of which he tied about his wrist. He tossed the ball on the floor, and then turned out the lights in the room, raised the shade of the window, and placed the bundle of blankets upon the sill.

"All ready," he said.

Bates put on the gloves and seized the rope, and Rodney adjusted the seat under his thighs. "You hold the blankets, if you will be so good, Mr. Montague, and keep them in place, if you can."

And Bates uncoiled some of the rope, and passed it over the top of the large bureau which stood beside the window. He brought the rope down to the middle of the body of the bureau, so that by this means he could diminish the pull of Rodney's weight.

"Steady, now," said the latter; and he climbed over the sill, and, holding on with his hands, gradually put his weight against the rope.

"Now! All ready," he whispered.

Bates grasped the line, and, bracing his knees against the bureau, paid the rope out inch by inch. Montague held the blankets in place in the corner, and Rodney's shoulders and head gradually disappeared below the sill. He was still holding on with his hands, however.

"All right," he whispered, and let go, and slowly the rope slid past.

Montague's heart was beating fast with excitement, but Bates was calm and businesslike. After he had let out several turns of the rope, he stopped and whispered, "Look out now."

Montague leaned over the sill. He could see a stream of light from the window below him. Rodney was standing upon the cornice at the top of the window.

"Lower," said Montague, as he drew in his head, and once more Bates paid out.

"Now," he whispered, and Montague looked again. Rodney had cleverly pushed himself by the corner of the cornice, and kept himself at one side of the window, so that he would not be visible from the inside of the room. He made a frantic signal with his hand, and Montague drew back and whispered, "Lower!"

The next time he looked out, Rodney was standing upon the sill of the window, leaning to one side.

"Now, make fast," muttered Bates. And while he held the rope, Montague took it and wound it again around the bureau, and then carried it over and made it fast to the leg of the bathtub.

"I guess that will hold all right," said Bates; and he went to the window and picked up the ball of cord, the other end of which was tied around Rodney's wrist.

"This is for signals," he said. "Morse telegraph."

"Good heavens!" gasped Montague. "You didn't leave much to chance."

"Couldn't afford to," said Bates. "Keep still!"

Montague saw that the hand which held the cord was being jerked.

"W-i-n-d-o-w o-p-e-n," said Bates; and added, "By the Lord! we've got them!"

CHAPTER XIX

Montague brought a couple of chairs, and the two seated themselves at the window for a long wait.

"How did you learn about this conference?" asked Montague.

"Be careful," whispered the other in his ear. "We mustn't make a noise, because Rodney will need quiet to hear them."

Montague saw that the cord was jerking again. Bates spelled out the letters one by one.

"W-a-t-e-r-m-a-n. D-u-v-a-l. He's telling us who's there. David Ward. Hegan. Prentice."

"Prentice!" whispered Montague. "Why, he's up in the Adirondacks!"

"He came down on a special train to-day," whispered the other. "Ward telegraphed him—I think that's where we got our tip. Henry Patterson. He's the real head of the Oil Trust now. Bascom of the Empire Bank. He's Waterman's man."

"You can imagine from that list that there's something big going on," Bates muttered; and he spelled the names of several other bankers, heads of the most important institutions in Wall Street.

"Talking about Stewart," spelled out Rodney.

"That's ancient history," muttered Bates. "He's a dead one."

"P-r-i-c-e," spelled Rodney.

"Price!" exclaimed Montague.

"Yes," said the other. "I saw him down in the lobby. I rather thought he'd come."

150

"But to a conference with Waterman!" exclaimed Montague.

"That's all right," said Bates. "Why not?"

"But they are deadly enemies!"

"Oh," said the other, "you don't want to let yourself believe things like that."

"What do you mean?" protested Montague. "Do you suppose they're not enemies?"

"I certainly do suppose it," said Bates.

"But, man! I can give you positive facts that prove they are."

"For every fact that you bring," laughed the other, "I can bring half a dozen to show you they are not."

"But that is perfectly absurd!" began Montague.

"Hush," said Bates, and he waited while the string jerked.

"I-c-e," spelled Rodney.

"That's Cummings—another dead one," said Bates. "My Lord, but they did him up brown!"

"Who did it?" asked Montague.

"Waterman," answered the other. "The Steamship Trust was competing with his New England railroads, and now it's in the hands of a receiver. Before long you'll hear that he's gathered it in."

"Then you think this last smash-up was planned?" said he.

"Planned! My Heavens, man, it was the greatest gobbling up of the little fish that I have ever known since I've been in Wall Street!"

"And it was Waterman?"

"With the Oil Trust. They were after young Stewart. You see, he beat them out in Montana, and they had to buy him off for ten million dollars. But he was fool enough to come to New York and go in for banking; and now they've got his banks, and a good part of his ten millions as well!"

"It takes a man's breath away," said Montague.

"Just save your breath—you'll need it to-night," said Bates, dryly.

The other sat in thought for a moment. "We were talking about Price," he whispered. "Do you mean John S. Price?"

"There is only one Price that I know of," was the reply.

"And you don't believe that he and Waterman are enemies?"

"I mean that Price is simply one of Waterman's agents in every big thing he does."

"But, man! Doesn't he own the Mississippi Steel Company?"

"He owns it for Waterman," said Bates.

"But that is impossible," cried Montague. "Isn't Waterman interested in the Steel Trust? And isn't Mississippi Steel its chief competitor?"

"It is supposed to be," said the other. "But that is simply a bluff to fool the public. There has been no real competition between them ever since four years ago, when Price raided the stock and captured it for Waterman."

Montague was staring at his friend, almost speechless with amazement.

"Mr. Bates," he said, "it happens that I was very recently connected with Price and the Mississippi Steel Company in a very intimate way; and I know most positively that what you say is not true."

"It's very hard to answer a statement like that," Bates responded. "I'd have to know just what your facts are. But they'd have to be very convincing indeed to make an impression upon me, for I ran that story down pretty thoroughly. I got it straight from the inside, and I got all the details of it. I nailed Price down, right in his own office. The only trouble was that my people wouldn't print the facts."

It was some time before Montague spoke again. He was groping round in his own mind, trying to grasp the significance of what Bates had said.

"But Price was fighting Waterman!" he whispered. "The whole crowd were fighting him! That was the whole purpose of what they were doing. It had no sense otherwise."

"But are you sure?" asked the other. "Think it over. Suppose they were only pretending to fight."

There was a silence again.

"Mind you," Bates added, "I am only speaking about Price himself. I don't know about any people he may have been with. He may have been deceiving them—he may have been leading them into a trap——"

And suddenly Montague clutched the arms of his chair. He sat staring ahead of him, struck dumb by the thought which the other's words had brought to him. "My God," he gasped; and again, and yet again, "My God!"

It seemed to unroll before him, in vista after vista. Price deceiving Ryder! leading him into that Northern Mississippi deal; getting him to lend money upon the stock of the Mississippi Steel Company; promising, perhaps, to support the stock in the market, and helping to smash it instead! Twisting Ryder round his finger, crushing him—and why? And why?

Montague's thoughts stopped still. It was as if he had found himself suddenly confronted by a bottomless abyss. He shrank back from it. He could not face the thought in his own mind. Waterman! It was Dan Waterman! It was something which he had planned! It was the vengeance that he had threatened! He had been all this time plotting it, setting his nets about Ryder's feet!

It was an idea so wild and so horrible that Montague fought it off. He pushed it away from him, again and again. No, no, it could not be!

And yet, why not? He had always felt certain in his own mind that that detective had come from Waterman. The old man had set to work to find out about Lucy and her affairs, the first time that he had ever laid eyes on her. And then suddenly Montague saw the face of volcanic fury that had flashed past him on board the *Brünnhilde*. "You will hear from me again," the old man had said; and now, all these months of silence—and at last he heard!

Why not? Why not? Montague kept asking himself. After all, what did he know about the Mississippi Steel Company? What had he ever seen to prove that it was actually competing with the Trust? What had he even heard, except what Stanley Ryder had told him; and what more likely than that Ryder was simply repeating what Price had said?

Montague had forgotten all about his present situation in the rush of thoughts which had come to him. The cord had been jerking again, and had spelled out the names of several more of the masters of the city who had arrived; but he had not heard their names. "What object would there be," he asked, "in keeping the fact a secret—I mean that Price was Waterman's agent?"

"Object!" exclaimed Bates. "Good heavens, and with the public half crazy about monopolies, and the President making such a fight! If it were known that the Steel Trust had gathered in its last big competitor, you can't tell what the Government might do!"

"I see," said Montague. "And how long has this been?"

"Four years," was the reply; "all they're waiting for is some occasion like this, when they can put the Company in a hole, and pose as benefactors in taking it over."

"I see," said Montague again.

"Listen," said Bates, and leaned out of the window. He could catch faintly the sounds of a deep voice in the consultation room.

"W-a-t-e-r-m-a-n," spelled Rodney.

"I guess business has begun," whispered Bates.

"Situation intolerable," spelled Rodney. "End wildcat banking."

"That means end of opposition to me," was the other's comment.

"Duval assents," continued Rodney.

The two in the window were on edge by this time. It was tantalizing to have to wait several minutes, and then get only such snatches.

"But they'll get past the speech-making pretty soon," whispered Bates; and indeed they did.

The next two words which the cord spelled out made Montague sit up and clutch the arms of his chair again.

"Gotham Trust!"

"Ah!" whispered Bates. Montague made not a sound.

"Ryder misusing," spelled the cord.

Bates seized his companion by the arm, and leaned close to him. "By the Lord!" he whispered breathlessly, "I wonder if they're going to smash the Gotham Trust!"

"Refuse clearing," spelled Rodney; and Montague felt Bates's hand trembling. "They refuse to clear for Ryder!" he panted.

Montague was beyond all speech; he sat as if turned to stone.

"To-morrow morning," spelled the cord.

Bates could hardly keep still for his excitement.

"Do you catch what that means?" he whispered. "The Clearing-house is to throw out the Gotham Trust!"

"Why, they'll wreck it!" panted the other.

"My God, my God, they're mad!" cried Bates. "Don't they realize what they'll do? There'll be a panic such as New York has never seen before! It will bring down every bank in the city! The Gotham Trust! Think of it!—the Gotham Trust!"

"Prentice objects," came Rodney's next message.

"Objects!" exclaimed Bates, striking his knee in repressed excitement. "I should think he might object. If the Gotham Trust goes down, the Trust Company of the Republic won't live for twenty-four hours."

"Afraid," spelled the cord. "Patterson angry."

"Much he has to lose," muttered Bates.

Montague started up, and began to pace the room. "Oh, this is horrible, horrible!" he exclaimed.

Through all the images of the destruction and suffering which Bates's words brought up before him, his thoughts flew back to a pale and sad-faced little woman, sitting alone in an apartment up on the Riverside. It was to her that it all came back; it was for her that this terrible drama was being enacted. Montague could picture the grim, hawk-faced old man, sitting at the head of the council board, and laying down the law to the masters of the Metropolis. And this man's thoughts, too, went back to Lucy—his and Montague's alone, of all those who took part in the struggle!

"Waterman protect Prentice," spelled Rodney. "Insist turn out Ryder. Withdraw funds."

"There's no doubt of it," whispered Bates; "they can finish him if they choose. But, oh, my Lord! what will happen in New York to-morrow?"

"Ward protect legitimate banks," was the next message.

"The little whelp!" sneered Bates. "By 'legitimate banks' he means those that back his syndicates. A lot of protecting he will do!"

But then the newspaper man in Bates rose to the surface. "Oh, what a story!" he whispered, clenching his hands, and pounding his knees—"oh, what a story!"

Montague carried away but a faint recollection of the rest of Rodney's communications; he was too much overwhelmed by his own thoughts. Bates, however, continued to spell out the words; and he caught the statement that General Prentice, who was a director in the Gotham Trust, was to vote against any plan to close the doors of that institution. While they were after it, they were going to finish it.

Also he caught the sentence, "Panic useful, curb President!" And he heard Bates's excited exclamations over that. "Did you catch that?" he cried. "That's Waterman! Oh, the nerve of it! We are in at the making of history to-night, Mr. Montague."

Perhaps half an hour later, Montague, standing beside Bates, saw his hand jerked violently several times.

"That means pull up!" cried he. "Quick!"

And he seized the rope. "Put your weight on it," he whispered. "It will hold."

They proceeded to haul. Rodney helped them by catching hold of the cornice of the window and lifting himself. Then there was a moment of great straining, during which Montague held his breath; after which the weight grew lighter again. Rodney had got his knees upon the cornice.

A few moments later his fingers appeared, clutching the edge of the sill. He swung himself up, and Montague and Bates grasped him under the arms, and fairly jerked him into the room.

He staggered to his feet; and there was a moment's pause, while all three caught their breath. Then Rodney leaped at Bates, and grasped him by the shoulders. "Old man!" he cried. "We landed them! We landed them!"

"We landed them!" laughed the other in exultation.

"Oh, what a scoop!" shouted Rodney. "There was never one like it."

The two were like schoolboys in their glee. They hugged each other, and laughed and danced about. But it was not long before they became serious again. Montague turned on the lights, and pulled down the window; and Rodney stood there, with his clothing dishevelled and his face ablaze with excitement, and talked to them.

"Oh, you can't imagine that scene!" he said. "It makes my hair stand on end to think of it. Just fancy—I was not more than twenty feet from Dan Waterman, and most of the time he seemed to be glaring right at me. I hardly dared wink, for fear he'd notice; and I thought every instant he would jump up and run to the window. But there he sat, and pounded on the table, and glared about at those fellows, and laid down the law to them."

"I've heard him talk," said Bates. "I know how it is."

"Why, he fairly knocked them over!" said the other. "You could have heard a pin drop when he got through. Oh, it was a mad thing to see!"

"I've hardly been able to get my breath," said Bates. "I can't believe it."

"They have no idea what it will mean," said Montague.

"They know," said Rodney; "but they don't care. They've smelt blood. That's about the size of it—they were like a lot of hounds on the trail. You should have seen Waterman, with that lean, hungry face of his. 'The time has come,' said he. 'There's no one here but has known that sooner or later this work had to be done. We must crush them, once and for all time!' And you should have seen him turn on Prentice, when he ventured a word."

"Prentice doesn't like it, then?" asked Montague.

"I should think he wouldn't!" put in Bates.

"Waterman said he'd protect him," said Rodney. "But he must place himself absolutely in their hands. It seems that the Trust Company of the Republic has a million dollars with the Gotham Trust, and that's to be withdrawn."

"Imagine it!" gasped Bates.

"And wait!" exclaimed the other; "then they got on to politics. I would have given one arm if I could have got a photograph of

Dan Waterman at that moment—just to spread it before the American people and ask them what they thought of it! David Ward had made the remark that 'A little trouble mightn't have a bad effect just now.' And Waterman brought down his fist on the table. 'This country needs a lesson,' he cried. 'There's been too much abuse of responsible men, and there's been too much wild talk in high places. If the people get a little taste of hard times, they'll have something else to think about besides abusing those who have made the prosperity of the country; and it seems to me, gentlemen, that we have it in our power to put an end to this campaign of Radicalism.'"

"Think of it, think of it!" gasped Bates. "The old devil!"

"And then Duval chimed in, with a laugh, 'To put it in a nutshell, gentlemen, we are going to smash Ryder and scare the President!'"

"Was the conference over?" asked Bates, after a moment's pause.

"All but the hand-shakes," said the other. "I didn't dare to stay while they were moving about."

And Bates started suddenly to his feet. "Come!" he said. "We haven't any time to waste. Our work isn't done yet, by a long sight."

He proceeded to untie the rope and coil it up. Rodney took the blanket and put it on the bed, covering it with the spread, so as to conceal the holes which had been worn by the rope. He wound up the ball of cord, and dropped it into the bag with the rest of the stuff. Bates took his hat and coat and started for the door.

"You will excuse us, Mr. Montague," he said. "You can understand that this story will need a lot of work."

"I understand," said Montague.

"We'll try to thank you by-and-by," added the other. "Come round after the paper goes to press, and we'll have a celebration."

CHAPTER XX

They went out; and Montague waited a minute or two, to give them a chance to get out of the way, and then he rang the elevator bell and entered the car.

It stopped again at the next floor, and he gave a start of excitement. As the door opened, he saw a group of men, with Duval, Ward, and General Prentice among them. He moved behind the elevator man, so that none of them should notice him.

Montague had caught one glimpse of the face of General Prentice. It was deathly pale. The General said not a word to anyone, but went out into the corridor. The other hesitated for a moment, then, with a sudden resolution, he turned and followed. As his friend passed out of the door, he stepped up beside him.

"Good-evening, General," he said. The General turned and stared at him, half in a daze.

"Oh, Montague!" he said. "How are you?"

"Very well," said Montague.

In the street outside, among a group of half a dozen automobiles, he recognized the General's limousine car.

"Where are you going?" he asked.

"Home," was the reply.

"I'll ride with you, if you like," said Montague. "I've something to say to you."

"All right," said the General. He could not very well have refused, for Montague had taken him by the arm and started toward the car; he did not intend to be put off.

He helped the General in, got in himself, and shut to the door behind him. Prentice sat staring in front of him, still half in a daze.

Montague watched him for a minute or so. Then suddenly he leaned toward him, and said, "General, why do you let them persuade you to do it?"

"Hey?" said the other.

"I say," repeated Montague, "why do you let them persuade you?"

The other turned and stared at him, with a startled look in his eyes.

"I know all about what has happened," said Montague. "I know what went on at that conference."

"What do you mean?" gasped the General.

"I know what they made you promise to do. They are going to wreck the Gotham Trust Company."

The General was dumfounded. "Why!" he gasped. "How? Who told you? How could you——"

Montague had to wait a minute or two until his friend had got over his dismay.

"I cannot help it," he burst out finally. "What can I do?"

"You can refuse to play their game!" exclaimed Montague.

"But don't you suppose that they would do it just the same? And how long do you suppose that I would last, if I refused them?"

"But think of what it means!" cried Montague. "Think of the ruin! You will bring everything about your head."

"I know, I know!" cried the General, in a voice of anguish. "Don't think that I haven't realized it—don't think that I haven't fought against it! But I am helpless, utterly helpless."

He turned upon Montague, and caught his sleeve with a trembling hand. "I never thought that I would live to face such an hour," he exclaimed. "To despise myself—to be despised by all the world! To be browbeaten, and insulted, and dragged about——"

The old man paused, choking with excess of emotion. "Look at me!" he cried, with sudden vehemence. "Look at me! You think that I am a man, a person of influence in the community, the head of a great institution in which thousands of

people have faith. But I am nothing of the kind. I am a puppet—I am a sham—I am a disgrace to myself and to the name
I bear!"

And suddenly he clasped his hands over his face, and bowed
his head, so that Montague should not see his grief.

There was a long silence. Montague was dumb with horror.
He felt that his mere presence was an outrage.

Finally the General looked up again. He clenched his hand,
and mastered himself.

"I have chosen my part," he said. "I must play it through.
What I feel about it makes no difference."

Montague again said nothing.

"I have no right to inflict my grief upon you," the General
continued. "I have no right to try to excuse myself. There is no
turning back now. I am Dan Waterman's man, and I do his bid-
ding."

"But how can you have got into such a position?" asked
Montague.

"A friend of mine organized the Trust Company of the
Republic. He asked me to become president, because I had a
name that would be useful to him. I accepted—he was a man I
knew I could trust. I managed the business properly, and it
prospered; and then, three years ago, the control was bought by
other men. That was when the crisis came. I should have
resigned. But I had my family to think of; I had friends who
were involved; I had interests that I could not leave. And I
stayed—and that is all. I found that I had stayed to be a puppet,
a figurehead. And now it is too late."

"But can't you withdraw now?" asked Montague.

"Now?" echoed the General—"now, in the most critical
moment, when all my friends are hanging upon me? There is
nothing that my enemies would like better, for they could lay all
their sins at my door. They would class me with Stewart and
Ryder."

"I see," said Montague, in a low voice.

"And now the crisis comes, and I find out who my real master
is. I am told to do this, and do that, and I do it. There are no
threats; I understand without any. Oh, my God, Mr. Montague,

if I should tell you of some of the things that I have seen in this city—of the indignities that I have seen heaped upon men, of the deeds to which I have seen them driven! Men whom you think of as the most honourable in the community—men who have grown grey in the service of the public! It is too brutal, too horrible for words!"

There was a long silence.

"And there is nothing you can do?" asked Montague.

"Nothing," he answered.

"Tell me, General, is your institution sound?"

"Perfectly sound."

"And you have done nothing improper?"

"Nothing."

"Then why should you fear Waterman?"

"Why?" exclaimed the General. "Because I am liable for eighty per cent of my deposits, and I have only five per cent of reserves."

"I see!" said Montague.

"It is a choice between Stanley Ryder and myself," added the other. "And Stanley Ryder will have to fight his own battle."

There was nothing more said. Each of the men sat buried in his own thoughts, and the only sound was the hum of the automobile as it sped up Broadway.

Montague was working out another course of action. He moved to another seat in the car where he could see the numbers upon the street lamps as they flashed by; and at last he touched the General upon the knee. "I will leave you at the next corner," he said.

The General pressed the button which signalled his chauffeur, and the car drew up at the curb. Montague descended.

"Good-night, General," he said.

"Good-night," said the other, in a faint voice. He did not offer to take Montague's hand. The latter closed the door of the car, and it sped away up the street.

Then he crossed over and went down to the River Drive, and entered Lucy's apartment house.

"Is Mrs. Taylor in?" he asked of the clerk.

"I'll see," said the man. Montague gave his name, and added, "Tell her it is very important."

Lucy came to the door herself, clad in an evening gown.

One glance at his haggard face was enough to tell her that something was wrong. "What is it, Allan?" she cried.

He hung up his hat and coat, and went into the drawing-room.

"What is it, Allan?" she cried again.

"Lucy, do you know where Stanley Ryder is?" he asked.

"Yes," she answered, and added quickly, "Oh! it's some bad news!"

"It is," said he. "He must be found at once."

She stared at him for a moment, hesitating; then, her anxiety overcoming every other emotion, she said, "He is in the next room."

"Call him," said Montague.

Lucy ran to the door. "Come in. Quickly!" she called, and Ryder appeared.

Montague saw that he was very pale; and there was nothing left of his air of aristocratic serenity.

"Mr. Ryder," he began, "I have just come into possession of some news which concerns you very closely. I felt that you ought to know. There is to be a directors' meeting to-morrow morning, at which it is to be decided that the bank which clears for the Gotham Trust Company will discontinue to do it."

Ryder started as if he had been shot; his face turned grey. There was no sound except a faint cry of fright from Lucy.

"My information is quite positive," continued Montague. "It has been determined to wreck your institution!"

Ryder caught at a chair to support himself. "Who? Who?" he stammered.

"It is Duval and Waterman," said Montague.

"Dan Waterman!" It was Lucy who spoke.

Montague turned to look at her, and saw her eyes, wide open with terror.

"Yes, Lucy," he said.

"Oh, oh!" she gasped, choking; then suddenly she cried wildly, "Tell me! I don't understand—what does it mean?"

"It means that I am ruined," exclaimed Ryder.

"Ruined?" she echoed.

"Absolutely!" he said. "They've got me! I knew they were after me, but I didn't think they'd dare!"

He ended with a furious imprecation; but Montague had kept his eyes fixed upon Lucy. It was her suffering that he cared about.

He heard her whisper, under her breath, "It's for me!" And then again, "It's for me!"

"Lucy," he began; but suddenly she put up her hand, and rushed toward him.

"Hush! he doesn't know!" she panted breathlessly. "I haven't told him."

And then she turned toward Ryder again. "Oh, surely there must be some way," she cried, wildly. "Surely——"

Ryder had sunk down in a chair and buried his face in his hands. "Ruined!" he exclaimed. "Utterly ruined! I won't have a dollar left in the world."

"No, no," cried Lucy, "it cannot be!" And she put her hands to her forehead, striving to think. "It must be stopped. I'll go and see him. I'll plead with him."

"You must not, Lucy!" cried Montague, starting toward her.

But again she whirled upon him. "Not a word!" she whispered, with fierce intensity. "Not a word!"

And she rushed into the next room, and half a minute later came back with her hat and wrap.

"Allan," she said, "tell them to call me a cab!"

He tried to protest again; but she would not hear him. "You can ride with me," she said. "You can talk then. Call me a cab! Please—save me that trouble."

He gave the message; and Lucy, meanwhile, stood in the middle of the room, twisting her hands together nervously.

"Now, Allan, go downstairs," she said; "wait for me there." And after another glance at the broken figure of Ryder, he took his hat and coat and obeyed.

Montague spent his time pacing back and forth in the entrance-hall. The cab arrived, and a minute later Lucy appeared, wearing a heavy veil. She went straight to the vehicle, and sprang in, and Montague followed. She gave the driver the address of Waterman's great marble palace over by the park; and the cab started.

Then suddenly she turned upon Montague, speaking swiftly and intensely.

"I know what you are going to say," she cried. "But you must spare me—and you must spare yourself. I am sorry that you should have to know this—God knows that I could not help it! But it cannot be undone. And there is no other way out of it. I must go to him, and try to save Ryder!"

"Lucy," he began, "listen to me——"

"I don't want to listen to you," she cried wildly—almost hysterically. "I cannot bear to be argued with. It is too hard for me as it is!"

"But think of the practical side of it!" he cried. "Do you imagine that you can stop this huge machine that Waterman has set in motion?"

"I don't know, I don't know!" she exclaimed, choking back a sob. "I can only do what I can. If he has any spark of feeling in him—I'll get down on my knees to him, I will beg him——"

"But, Lucy! think of what you are doing. You go there to his house at night! You put yourself into his power!"

"I don't care, Allan—I am not afraid of him. I have thought about myself too long. Now I must think about the man I love."

Montague did not answer for a moment. "Lucy," he said at last, "will you tell me how you have thought of yourself in one single thing?"

"Yes, yes—I will!" she cried vehemently. "I have known all along that Waterman was following me. I have been haunted by the thought of him—I have felt his power in everything that has befallen us. And I have never once told Ryder of his peril!"

"That was more a kindness to him——" began the other.

"No, no!" panted Lucy; and she caught his coat-sleeve in her trembling hands. "You see, you see—you cannot even imagine it of me! I kept it a secret—because I was afraid!"

"Afraid?" he echoed.

"I was afraid that Ryder would leave me! I was afraid that he would give me up! And I loved him too much!—Now," she rushed on—"you see what kind of a person I have been! And I can sit here, and tell you that! Is there anything that can make me ashamed after that? Is there anything that can degrade me after that? And what is there left for me to do but go to Waterman and try to undo what I have done?"

Montague was speechless, before the agony of her humiliation.

"You see!" she whispered.

"Lucy," he began, protesting.

But suddenly she caught him by the arm. "Allan," she whispered, "I know that you have to try to stop me. But it is no use, and I must do it! And I cannot bear to hear you—it makes it too hard for me. My course is chosen, and nothing in the world can turn me; and I want you to go away and leave me. I want you to go—right now! I am not afraid of Waterman; I am not afraid of anything that he can do. I am only afraid of you, and your unhappiness. I want you to leave me to my fate! I want you to stop thinking about me!"

"I cannot do it, Lucy," he said.

She reached up and pulled the signal-cord; and the cab came to a halt.

"I want you to get out, Allan!" she cried wildly. "Please get out, and go away."

He started to protest again; but she pushed him away in frenzy. "Go, go!" she cried; and half dazed, and scarcely realizing what he did, he gave way to her and stepped out into the street.

"Drive!" she called to the man, and shut the door; and Montague found himself standing on a drive in the park, with the lights of the cab disappearing round a turn.

CHAPTER XXI

Montague started to walk. He had no idea where he went; his mind was in a whirl, and he was lost to everything about him. He must have spent a couple of hours wandering about the park and the streets of the city; when at last he stopped and looked about him, he was on a lighted thoroughfare, and a big clock in front of a jewellery store was pointing to the hour of two.

He looked around. Immediately across the street was a building which he recognized as the office of the *Express*, and in a flash he thought of Bates. "Come in after the paper has gone to press," the latter had said.

He went in and entered the elevator.

"I want to see Mr. Bates, a reporter," he said.

"City-room," said the elevator man; "eleventh floor."

Montague confronted a very cross and sleepy-looking office-boy. "Is Mr. Bates in?" he asked.

"I dunno," said the boy, and slowly let himself down from the table upon which he had been sitting. Montague produced a card, and the boy disappeared. "This way," he said, when he returned; and Montague found himself in a huge room, crowded with desks and chairs. Everything was in confusion; the floor was literally buried out of sight in paper.

Montague observed that there were only about a dozen men in the room; and several of these were putting on their coats. "There he is, over there," said the office-boy.

He looked and saw Bates sitting at a desk, with his head buried in his arms. "Tired," he thought to himself.

"Hello, Bates," he said; then, as the other looked up, he gave a start of dismay.

"What's the matter?" he cried.

It was half a minute before Bates replied. His voice was husky. "They sold me out," he whispered.

"What!" gasped the other.

"They sold me out!" repeated Bates, and struck the table in front of him. "Cut out the story, by God! Did me out of my scoop!"

"Look at that, sir," he added, and shoved toward Montague a double column of newspaper proofs, with a huge headline, "Gotham Trust Company to be Wrecked," and the words scrawled across in blue pencil, "Killed by orders from the office."

Montague could scarcely find words to reply. He drew up a chair and sat down. "Tell me about it," he said.

"There's nothing much to tell," said Bates. "They sold me out. They wouldn't print it."

"But why didn't you take it elsewhere?" asked the other.

"Too late," said Bates; "the scoundrels—they never even let me know!" He poured out his rage in a string of curses.

Then he told Montague the story.

"I was in here at half-past ten," he said, "and I reported to the managing editor. He was crazy with delight, and told me to go ahead—front page, double column, and all the rest. So Rodney and I set to work. He did the interview, and I did all the embroidery—oh, my God, but it was a story! And it was read, and went through; and then an hour or two ago, just when the formes were ready, in comes old Hodges—he's one of the owners, you know—and begins nosing round. 'What's this?' he cries, and reads the story; and then he goes to the managing editor. They almost had a fight over it. 'No paper that I am interested in shall ever print a story like that!' says Hodges; and the managing editor threatens to resign, but he can't budge him. The first thing I knew of it was when I got this copy; and the paper had already gone to press."

"What do you suppose was the reason for it?" asked Montague, in wonder.

"Reason?" echoed Bates. "The reason is Hodges; he's a crook. 'If we publish that story,' he said, 'the directors of the bank will never meet, and we'll bear the onus of having wrecked the Gotham Trust Company.' But that's all a bluff, and he knew it; we could prove that that conference took place, if it ever came to a fight."

"You were quite safe, it seems to me," said Montague.

"Safe?" echoed Bates. "We had the greatest scoop that a newspaper ever had in this country—if only the *Express* were a newspaper. But Hodges isn't publishing the news, you see; he's serving his masters, whoever they are. I knew that it meant trouble when he bought into the *Express*. He used to be managing editor of the *Gazette,* you know; and he made his fortune selling the policy of that paper—its financial news is edited to this very hour in the offices of Wyman's bankers, and I can prove it to anybody who wants me to. That's the sort of proposition a man's up against; and what's the use of gathering the news?"

And Bates rose up with an oath, kicking away the chair behind him. "Come on," he said; "let's get out of here. I don't know that I'll ever come back."

Montague spent another hour wandering about with Bates, listening to his opinion of the newspapers of the Metropolis. Then, utterly exhausted, he went home; but not to sleep. He sat in a chair for an hour or two, his mind besieged by images of ruin and destruction. At last he lay down, but he had not closed his eyes when daylight began to stream into the room.

At eight o'clock he was up again and at the telephone. He called up Lucy's apartment house.

"I want to speak to Mrs. Taylor," he said.

"She is not in," was the reply.

"Will you ring up the apartment?" asked Montague. "I will speak to the maid."

"This is Mr. Montague," he said, when he heard the woman's voice. "Where is Mrs. Taylor?"

"She has not come back, sir," was the reply.

Montague had some work before him that day which

could not be put off. Accordingly he bathed and shaved, and had some coffee in his room, and then set out for his office. Even at that early hour there were crowds in the financial district, and another day's crop of rumours had begun to spring. He heard nothing about the Gotham Trust Company; but when he left court at lunch-time, the newsboys on the street were shouting the announcement of the action of the bank directors. Lucy had failed in her errand, then; the blow had fallen!

There was almost a panic on the Exchange that day, and the terror and anxiety upon the faces of the people who thronged the financial district were painful to see. But the courts did not suspend, even on account of the Gotham Trust; and Montague had an important case to argue. He came out on the street late in the afternoon, and though it was after banking hours he saw crowds in front of a couple of the big trust companies, and he read in the papers that a run upon the Gotham Trust had begun.

At his office he found a telegram from his brother Oliver, who was still in the Adirondacks: "Money in Trust Company of the Republic. Notify me of the slightest sign of trouble."

He replied that there was none; and, as he rode up in the subway, he thought the problem over, and made up his own mind. He had a trifle over sixty thousand dollars in Prentice's institution—more than half of all he owned. He had Prentice's word for it that the Company was in a sound condition, and he believed it. He made up his mind that he would not be one of those to be stampeded whatever might happen.

He dined quietly at home with his mother; then he took his way up town again to Lucy's apartment; for he was haunted by the thought of her, and could not rest. He had read in the late evening papers that Stanley Ryder had resigned from the Gotham Trust Company.

"Is Mrs. Taylor in?" he asked, and gave his name.

"Mrs. Taylor says will you please to wait, sir," was the reply. And Montague sat down in the reception-room. A couple of minutes later, the hall-boy brought him a note.

He opened it and read these words, in a trembling hand:

"Dear Allan,

It is good of you to try to help me, but I cannot bear it. Please go away. I do not want you to think about me.

"Lucy."

Montague could read the agony between those lines; but there was nothing he could do about it. He went over to Broadway, and started to walk down town.

He felt that he must have someone to talk to, to take his mind off these things. He thought of the Major, and went over to the club, but the storm had routed out even the Major, it appeared. He was just off to attend some conference, and had only time to shake hands with Montague, and tell him to "trim sail."

Then he thought of Bates, and went down to the office of the *Express*. He found Bates hard at work, seated at a table in his shirt-sleeves, and with stacks of papers round him.

"I can always spare time for a chat," he said, as Montague offered to go.

"I see you came back," observed the other.

"I'm like an old horse in a tread-mill," answered Bates. "What else is there for me to do?"

He leaned back in his chair, and put his thumbs in his arm-holes. "Well," he remarked, "they made their killing."

"They did, indeed," said Montague.

"And they're not satisfied yet," exclaimed the other. "They're on another trail!"

"What!" cried Montague.

"Listen," said Bates. "I went in to see David Ward about the action of the Clearing-house Committee; Gary—he's the *Despatch* man—was with me. Ward talked for half an hour, as he always does; he told us all about the gallant efforts which the bankers were making to stem the tide, and he told us that the Trust Company of the Republic was in danger, and that an agreement had been made to try to save it. Mind you, there's not been the least sign of trouble for the company. 'Shall we print that?' asked Gary. 'Surely,' said Ward. 'But it will make trouble,' said Gary. 'That's all right,' said Ward. 'It's a fact. So print it.' Now, what do you think of that?"

Montague sat rigid. "But I thought they had promised to protect Prentice!" he exclaimed.

"Yes," said Bates grimly; "and now they throw him down."

"Do you suppose Waterman knew that?"

"Why, of course; Ward is no more than one of his clerks."

"And will the *Despatch* print it, do you suppose?"

"I don't know why not," said the other. "I asked Gary if he was going to put it in, and he said 'Yes.' 'It will make another panic,' I said, and he answered, 'Panics are news.'"

Montague said nothing for a minute or two. Finally he remarked, "I have good reason to believe that the Trust Company of the Republic is perfectly sound."

"I have no doubt of it," was the reply.

"Then why——" He stopped.

Bates shrugged his shoulders. "Ask Waterman," he said. "It's some quarrel or other; he wants to put the screws on somebody. Perhaps it's simply that two trust companies will scare the President more than one; or perhaps it's some stock he wants to break. I've heard it said that he has seventy-five millions laid by to pick up bargains with; and I shouldn't wonder if it was true."

There was a moment's pause. "And by the way," Bates added, "the Oil Trust has made another haul! The Electric Manufacturing Company is in trouble—that's a rival of one of their enterprises! Doesn't it all fit together beautifully?"

Montague thought for a moment or two. "This is rather important news to me," he said; "I've got money in the Trust Company of the Republic. Do you suppose they are going to let it go down?"

"I talked it over with Rodney," the other replied. "He says Waterman was quite explicit in his promises to see Prentice through. And there's one thing you can say about old Dan—for all his villainies, he never breaks his word. So I imagine he'll save it."

"But then, why give out this report?" exclaimed the lawyer.

"Don't you see?" said Bates. "He wants a chance to save it."

Montague's jaw fell. "Oh!" he said.

"It's as plain as the nose on your face," said Bates. "That story will come out to-morrow morning, and everybody will say it was the blunder of a newspaper reporter; and then Waterman will come forward and do the rescue act. It'll be just like a play."

"It's taking a long chance," said Montague, and added, "I had thought of telling Prentice, who's an intimate friend of mine; but I don't suppose it will do him any good."

"Poor old Prentice can't help himself," was the reply. "All you can do is to make him lose a night's sleep."

Montague went out, with a new set of problems to ponder. As he went home, he passed the magnificent building of the Gotham Trust Company, where there stood a long line of people who had prepared to spend the night. All the afternoon a frantic mob had besieged the doors, and millions of dollars had been withdrawn in a few hours. Montague knew that by the time he got to town the next morning there would be another such mob in front of the Trust Company of the Republic; but he was determined to stand by his own resolve. However, he had sent a telegram to Oliver, warning him to return at once.

He went home, and found there another letter from Lucy Dupree.

"DEAR ALLAN" (she wrote),

"No doubt you have heard the news that Ryder has been forced out of the Gotham Trust. But I have accomplished part of my purpose—Waterman has promised that he will put him on his feet again after this trouble is over. In the meantime, I am told to go away. This is for the best; you will remember that you yourself urged me to go. Ryder cannot see me, because the newspaper reporters are following him so closely.

"I beg of you not to try to find me. I am hateful in my own sight, and you will never see me again. There is one last thing that you can do for me. Go to Stanley Ryder and offer him your help—I mean your advice in straightening out his affairs. He has no friends now, and he is in a desperate plight. Do this for me.
                                                                "LUCY."

CHAPTER XXII

At eight the next morning the train from the Adirondacks arrived, and Montague was awakened by his brother at the telephone. "Have you seen this morning's *Despatch?*" was Oliver's first word.

"I haven't seen it," said Montague; "but I know what's in it."

"About the Trust Company of the Republic?" asked Oliver.

"Yes," said the other. "I was told the story before I telegraphed you."

"But, my God, man," cried Oliver—"then why aren't you in town?"

"I'm going to let my money stay."

"What?"

"I believe that the institution is sound; and I am not going to leave Prentice in the lurch. I telegraphed you, so that you could do as you chose."

It was a moment or two before Oliver could find words to reply.

"Thanks!" he said. "You might have done a little more—sent somebody down to keep a place in line for me. You're out of your mind, but there's no time to talk about it now. Good-bye." And so he rang off.

Montague dressed and had his breakfast; in the meantime he glanced over a copy of the *Despatch,* where, in the account of the day's events, he found the fatal statements about the Trust Company of the Republic. It was very interesting to Montague to read these newspapers and see the picture of events which they presented to the public. They all told what they could not avoid telling—that is, the events which were public matters; but they never by any chance gave a hint of the reasons for the happenings—you would have supposed that all these upheavals in the banking world were so many thunderbolts which had fallen from the heavens above. And each day they gave more of their space to insisting that the previous day's misfortunes were the last—that by no chance could there be any more thunderbolts to fall.

When he went down town, he rode one station farther than usual in order to pass the Trust Company of the Republic. He found a line of people extending half-way round the block, and in the minute that he stood watching there were a score or more added to it. Police were patrolling up and down—it was not many hours later that they were compelled to adopt the expedient of issuing numbered tickets to those who waited in the line.

Montague walked on toward the front, looking for his brother. But he had not gone very far before he gave an exclamation of amazement. He saw a short, stout, grey-haired figure, which he recognized, even by its back. "Major Venable!" he gasped.

The Major whirled about. "Montague!" he exclaimed. "My God, you are just in time to save my life!"

"What do you want?" asked the other.

"I want a chair!" gasped the Major, whose purple features seemed about to burst with his unwonted exertions. "I've been standing here for two hours. In another minute more I should have sat down on the sidewalk."

"Where can I get a chair?" asked Montague, biting his tongue in order to repress his amusement.

"Over in Broadway," said the Major. "Go into one of the stores, and make somebody sell you one. Pay anything—I don't care."

So Montague went back, and entered a leather-goods store, where he saw several cane-seated chairs. He was free to laugh then all he pleased; and he explained the situation to one of the clerks, who demurred at five dollars, but finally consented for ten dollars to take the risk of displeasing his employer. For fifty cents more Montague found a boy to carry it, and he returned in triumph to his venerable friend.

"I never expected to see you in a position like this," he remarked. "I thought you always knew things in advance."

"By the Lord, Montague!" muttered the other, "I've got a quarter of a million in this place."

"I've got about one-fourth as much myself," said Montague.

"What!" cried the Major. "Then what are you doing?"

"I'm going to leave it in," said Montague. "I have reason to know that that report in the *Despatch* is simply a blunder, and that the institution is sound."

"But, man, there'll be a run on it!" sputtered the old gentleman.

"There will, if everybody behaves like you. You don't need your quarter of a million to pay for your lunch, do you?"

The Major was too much amazed to find a reply.

"You put your money in a trust company," the other continued, "and you know that it only keeps five per cent reserve, and is liable to pay a hundred per cent of its deposits. How can you expect it to do that?"

"I don't expect it," said the Major grimly; "I expect to be among the five per cent." And he cast his eye up the line, and added, "I rather think I am."

Montague went on ahead, and found his brother, with only about a score of people ahead of him. Apparently not many of the depositors of the Trust Company read their newspapers before eight o'clock in the morning.

"Do you want a chair, too?" asked Montague. "I just got one for the Major."

"Is he here, too?" exclaimed Oliver. "Good heavens! No, I don't want a chair," he added, "I'll get through early. But, Allan, tell me—what in the world is the matter. Do you really mean that your money is still in here?"

"It's here," the other answered. "There's no use arguing about it—come over to the office when you get your money."

"I got the train just by half a minute," said Oliver. "Poor Bertie Stuyvesant didn't get up in time, and he's coming on a special—he's got about three hundred thousand in here. It was to pay for his new yacht."

"I guess some of the yacht-makers won't be quite so busy from now," remarked the other, as he moved away.

That afternoon he heard the story of how General Prentice, as a director of the Gotham Trust, had voted that the institution should not close its doors, and then, as president of the Trust Company of the Republic, had sent over and cashed a cheque for a million dollars. None of the newspapers printed that story, but it ran from mouth to mouth, and was soon the jest of the whole city. Men said that it was this act of treachery which had taken the heart out of the Gotham Trust Company directors, and led to the closing of its doors.

Such was the beginning of the panic as Montague saw it. It had all worked out beautifully, according to the schedule. The stock market was falling to pieces—some of the leading stocks were falling several points between transactions, and Wyman and Hegan and the Oil and Steel people were hammering the market and getting ready for the killing. And at the same time, representatives of Waterman in Washington were interviewing the President, and setting before him the desperate plight of the Mississippi Steel Company. Already the structure of the country's finances was tottering; and here was one more big failure threatening. Realizing the desperate situation, the Steel Trust was willing to do its part to save the country—it would take over the Mississippi Steel Company, provided only that the Government would not interfere. The desired promise was given; and so that last of Waterman's purposes was accomplished.

But there was one factor in the problem upon which few had reckoned, and that was the vast public which furnished all the money for the game—the people to whom dollars were not simply gamblers' chips, but to whom they stood for the necessities of life; business men who must have them to pay their clerks on Saturday afternoon; working men who needed them for rent and food; helpless widows and orphans to whom they meant safety from starvation. These unhappy people had no means of knowing that financial institutions, which were perfectly sound and able to pay their depositors, might be wrecked deliberately in a gamblers' game. When they heard that banks were tottering, and were being besieged for money, they concluded that there must be real danger—that the long-predicted crash must be at hand. They descended upon Wall Street in hordes—the whole financial district was packed with terrified crowds, and squads of policemen rode through upon horseback in order to keep open the streets.

"Somebody asked for a dollar," was the way one banker phrased it. Wall Street had been doing business with pieces of paper; and now someone asked for a dollar, and it was discovered that the dollar had been mislaid.

It was an experience for which the captains of finance were not entirely prepared; they had forgotten the public. It was like some great convulsion of Nature, which made mockery of all the powers of men, and left the beholder dazed and terrified. In Wall Street men stood as if in a valley, and saw far up above them the starting of an avalanche; they stood fascinated with horror, and watched it gathering headway; saw the clouds of dust rising up, and heard the roar of it swelling, and realized that it was a matter of only a second or two before it would be upon them and sweep them to destruction.

The lines of people before the Gotham Trust and the Trust Company of the Republic were now blocks in length; and every hour one heard of runs upon new institutions. There were women wringing their hands and crying in nervous excitement; there were old people, scarcely able to totter; there were people who had risen from sick-beds, and who stood all through the day and night, shivering in the keen October winds.

Runs had begun on the savings banks also; over on the East Side the alarm had reached the ignorant foreign population. It had spread with the speed of lightning all over the country; already there were reports of runs in other cities, and from thousands and tens of thousands of banks in East and South and West came demands upon the Metropolis for money. And there was no money anywhere.

And so the masters of the Banking Trust realized to their annoyance that the monster which they had turned loose might get beyond their control. Runs were beginning upon institutions in which they themselves were concerned. In the face of madness such as this, even the twenty-five per cent reserves of the national banks would not be sufficient. The moving of the cotton and grain crops had taken hundreds of millions from New York; and there was no money to be got by any chance from abroad. Everywhere they turned, they faced this appalling scarcity of money; nothing could be sold, no money could be borrowed. The few who had succeeded in getting their cash were renting safe-deposit boxes and hiding the actual coin.

And so, all their purposes having been accomplished, the bankers set to work to stem the tide. Frantic telegrams were sent to Washington, and the Secretary of the Treasury deposited six million dollars in the national banks of the Metropolis, and then came on himself to consult.

Men turned to Dan Waterman, who was everywhere recognized as the master of the banking world. The rivalry of the different factions ceased in the presence of this peril; and Waterman became suddenly a king, with practically absolute control of the resources of every bank in the city. Even the Government placed itself in his hands; the Secretary of the Treasury became one of his clerks, and bank presidents and financiers came crowding into his office like panic-stricken children. Even the proudest and most defiant men, like Wyman and Hegan, took his orders and listened humbly to his tirades.

All these events were public history, and one might follow them day by day in the newspapers. Waterman's earlier acts had been planned and carried out in darkness. No one knew, no one had the faintest suspicion. But now newspaper reporters attended the conferences and trailed Waterman about wherever he went, and the public was invited to the wonderful spectacle of this battle-worn veteran, rousing himself for one last desperate campaign and saving the honour and credit of the country.

The public hung upon his lightest word, praying for his success. The Secretary of the Treasury sat in the Sub-Treasury building near his office and poured out the funds of the Government under his direction. Thirty-two million dollars in all were thus placed with the national banks; and from all these institutions Waterman drew the funds which he poured into the vaults of the imperilled banks and trust companies. It was a time when one man's peril was every man's, and none might stand alone. And Waterman was a despot, imperious and terrible. "I have taken care of my bank," said one president; "and I intend to shut myself up in it and wait until the storm is over." "If you do," Waterman retorted, "I will build a wall around you, and you will never get out of it again!" And so the banker contributed the necessary number of millions.

The fight centred around the imperilled Trust Company of the Republic. It was recognized by everyone that if Prentice's institution went down, it would mean defeat. Longer and longer grew the line of waiting depositors; the vaults were nearly empty. The cashiers adopted the expedient of paying very slowly—they would take half an hour or more to investigate a single cheque; and thus they kept going until more money arrived. The savings banks of the city agreed unanimously to close their doors, availing themselves of their legal right to demand sixty days before paying. The national banks resorted to the expedient of paying with clearing-house certificates. The newspapers preached confidence and cheered the public—even the newsboys were silenced, so that their shrill cries might no longer increase the public excitement. Groups of mounted policemen swept up and down the streets, keeping the crowds upon the move.

And so at last came the fateful Thursday, the climax of the panic. A pall seemed to have fallen upon Wall Street. Men ran here and there, bareheaded and pale with fright. Upon the floor of the Stock Exchange men held their breath. The market was falling to pieces. All sales had stopped; one might quote any price one chose, for it was impossible to borrow a dollar. Interest rates had gone to one hundred and fifty per cent to two hundred per cent; a man might have offered a thousand per cent for a large sum and not obtained it. The brokers stood about, gazing at each other in utter despair. Such an hour had never before been known.

All this time the funds of the Government had been withheld from the Exchange. The Government must not help the gamblers, everyone insisted. But now had come the moment when it seemed that the Exchange must be closed. Thousands of firms would be ruined, the business of the country would be paralyzed. There came word that the Pittsburg Exchange had closed. So once more the terrified magnates crowded into Waterman's office. Once more the funds of the Government were poured into the banks; and from the banks they came to Waterman; and within a few minutes after the crisis had developed, the announcement was made that Dan Waterman would lend twenty-five million dollars at ten per cent.

So the peril was averted. Brokers upon the floor wept for joy, and cheers rang through all the Street. A mob of men gathered in front of Waterman's office, singing a chorus of adulation.

All these events Montague followed day by day. He was passing through Wall Street that Thursday afternoon, and he heard the crowds singing. He turned away, bitter and sick at heart. Could a more tragic piece of irony have been imagined than this—that the man, who of all men had been responsible for this terrible calamity, should be heralded before the whole country as the one who averted it? Could there have been a more appalling illustration of the way in which the masters of the Metropolis were wont to hoodwink its blind and helpless population?

There was only one man to whom Montague could vent his feelings; only one man besides himself who knew the real truth. Montague got the habit, when he left his work, of stopping at the *Express* building, and listening for a few minutes to the grumbling of Bates.

Bates would have each day's news fresh from the inside; not only the things which would be printed on the morrow, but the things which would never be printed anywhere. And he and Montague would feed the fires of each other's rage. One day it would be one of the *Express*'s own editorials, in which it was pointed out that the intemperate speeches and reckless policies of the President were now bearing their natural fruit; another day it would be a letter from a prominent clergyman, naming Waterman as the President's successor.

Men were beside themselves with wonder at the generosity of

Waterman in lending twenty-five millions at ten per cent. But it
was not his own money—it was the money of the national banks
which he was lending; and this was money which the national
banks had got from the Government, and for which they paid
the Government no interest at all. There was never any graft in
the world so easy as the national bank graft, declared Bates.
These smooth gentlemen got the people's money to build their
institutions. They got the Government to deposit money with
them, and they paid the Government nothing, and charged the
people interest for it. They had the privilege of issuing a few
hundred millions of bank-notes, and they charged interest for
these, and paid the Government nothing. And then, to cap the
climax, they used their profits to buy up the Government! They
filled the Treasury Department with their people, and when
they got into trouble, the Sub-Treasury was emptied into their
vaults. And in the face of all this, the people agitated for postal
savings banks, and couldn't get them. In other countries the
people had banks where they could put their money with absolute certainty; for no one had ever known such a thing as a run
upon a postal bank.

"Sometimes," said Bates, "it seems almost as if our people
were hypnotized. You saw all this life insurance scandal, Mr.
Montague; and there's one simple and obvious remedy for all
the evils—if we had Government life insurance, it could never
fail, and there'd be no surplus for Wall Street gamblers. It
sounds almost incredible—but, do you know, I followed that
agitation as I don't believe any other man in this country followed it—and from first to last I don't believe that one single
suggestion of that remedy was ever made in print!"

A startled look had come upon Montague's face as he listened. "I don't believe I ever thought of it myself!" he
exclaimed.

And Bates shrugged his shoulders. "You see!" he said. "So it
goes."

CHAPTER XXIII

Montague had taken a couple of days to think over Lucy's last request. It was a difficult commission; but he made up his mind at last that he would make the attempt. He went up to Ryder's home and presented his card.

"Mr. Ryder is very much occupied, sir——" began the butler apologetically.

"This is important," said Montague. "Take him the card, please." He waited in the palatial entrance-hall, decorated with ceilings which had been imported intact from old Italian palaces.

At last the butler returned. "Mr. Ryder says will you please see him upstairs, sir?"

Montague entered the elevator, and was taken to Ryder's private apartments. In the midst of the drawing-room was a great library table, covered with a mass of papers; and in a chair in front of it sat Ryder.

Montague had never seen such dreadful suffering upon a human countenance. The exquisite man of fashion had grown old in a week.

"Mr. Ryder," he began, when they were alone, "I received a letter from Mrs. Taylor, asking me to come to see you."

"I know," said Ryder. "It was like her; and it is very good of you."

"If there is any way that I can be of assistance," the other began.

But Ryder shook his head. "No," he said "there is nothing."

"If I could give you my help in straightening out your own affairs——"

"They are beyond all help," said Ryder. "I have nothing to begin on—I have not a dollar in the world."

"That is hardly possible," objected Montague.

"It is literally true!" he exclaimed. "I have tried every plan—I have been over the thing and over it, until I am almost out of my mind." And he glanced about him at the confusion of papers, and leaned his forehead in his hands in despair.

"Perhaps if a fresh mind were to take it up," suggested Montague. "It is difficult to see how a man of your resources could be left without anything——"

"Everything I have is mortgaged," said the other. "I have been borrowing money right and left. I was counting on profits—I was counting on increases in value. And now see—everything is wiped out! There is not value enough left in anything to cover the loans."

"But, surely, Mr. Ryder, this slump is merely temporary. Values must be restored——"

"It will be years—it will be years! And in the meantime I shall be forced to sell. They have wiped me out—they have destroyed me! I have not even money to live on."

Montague sat for a few moments in thought. "Mrs. Taylor wrote me that Waterman——" he began.

"I know, I know!" cried the other. "He had to tell her something, to get what he wanted."

Montague said nothing.

"And suppose he does what he promised?" continued the other. "He has done it before—but am I to be one of Dan Waterman's lackeys?"

There was a silence. "Like John Lawrence," continued Ryder, in a low voice. "Have you heard of Lawrence? He was a banker—one of the oldest in the city. And Waterman gave him an order, and he defied him. Then he broke him; took away every dollar he owned. And the man came to him on his knees. 'I've taught you who is your master,' said Waterman. 'Now here's your money.' And now Lawrence fawns on him, and he's got rich and fat. But all his bank exists for is to lend money when Waterman is floating a merger, and call it in when he is buying."

Montague could think of nothing to reply to that.

"Mr. Ryder," he began at last, "I cannot be of much use to you now, because I haven't the facts. All I can tell you is that I am at your disposal. I will give you my best efforts, if you will let me. That is all I can say."

And Ryder looked up, the light shining on his white, wan face. "Thank you, Mr. Montague," he said. "It is very good of you. It is a help, at least, to hear a word of sympathy. I—I will let you know——"

"All right," said Montague, rising. He put out his hand, and Ryder took it tremblingly. "Thank you," he said again.

And the other turned and went out. He went down the great staircase by himself. At the foot he passed the butler, carrying a tray with some coffee.

He stopped the man. "Mr. Ryder ought not to be left alone," he said. "He should have his physician."

"Yes, sir," began the other, and then stopped short. From the floor above a pistol shot rang out and echoed through the house.

"Oh, my God!" gasped the butler, staggering backward.

He half dropped and half set the tray upon a chair, and ran wildly up the steps. Montague stood for a moment or two as if turned to stone. He saw another servant run out of the dining-room and up the stairs. Then, with a sudden impulse, he turned and went to the door.

"I can be of no use," he thought to himself; "I should only drag Lucy's name into it." And he opened the door, and went quietly down the steps.

In the newspapers the next morning he read that Stanley Ryder had shot himself in the body, and was dying.

And that same morning the newspapers in Denver, Colorado, told of the suicide of a mysterious woman, a stranger, who had gone to a room in one of the hotels and taken poison. She was very beautiful; it was surmised that she must be an actress. But she had left not a scrap of paper or a clue of any sort by which she could be identified. The newspapers printed her photograph; but Montague did not see the Denver newspapers, and so to the day of his death he never knew what had been the fate of Lucy Dupree.

The panic was stopped, but the business of the country lay in ruins. For a week its financial heart had ceased to beat, and through all the arteries of commerce, and every smallest capillary, there was stagnation. Hundreds of firms had failed, and the mills and factories by the thousands were closing down. There were millions of men out of work. Throughout the summer the railroads had been congested with traffic, and now there were a quarter of a million freight cars laid by. Everywhere were poverty and suffering; it was as if a gigantic tidal wave of distress had started from the Metropolis and rolled over the continent. Even the oceans had not stopped it; it had gone on to England and Germany—it had been felt even in South America and Japan.

One day, while Montague was still trembling with the pain of his experience, he was walking up the Avenue, and he met Laura Hegan coming from a shop to her carriage.

"Mr. Montague," she exclaimed, and stopped with a frank smile of greeting. "How are you?"

"I am well," he answered.

"I suppose," she added, "you have been very busy these terrible days."

"I have been more busy observing than doing," he replied.

"And how is Alice?"

"She is well. I suppose you have heard that she is engaged."

"Yes," said Miss Hegan. "Harry told me the first thing. I was perfectly delighted."

"Are you going up town?" she added. "Get in and drive with me."

He entered the carriage, and they joined the procession up the Avenue. They talked for a few minutes, then suddenly Miss Hegan said, "Won't you and Alice come to dinner with us some evening this week?"

Montague did not answer for a moment.

"Father is home now," Miss Hegan continued. "We should like so much to have you."

He sat staring in front of him. "No," he said at last, in a low voice. "I would rather not come."

His manner, even more than his words, struck his companion. She glanced at him in surprise.

"Why?" she began, and stopped. There was a silence.

"Miss Hegan," he said at last, "I might make conventional excuses. I might say that I have engagements; that I am very busy. Ordinarily one does not find it worth while to tell the truth in this social world of ours. But somehow I feel impelled to deal frankly with you."

He did not look at her. Her eyes were fixed upon him in wonder. "What is it?" she asked.

And he replied, "I would rather not meet your father again."

"Why? Has anything happened between you and father?" she exclaimed in dismay.

"No," he answered; "I have not seen your father since I had lunch with you in Newport."

"Then what is it?"

He paused a moment. "Miss Hegan," he began, "I have had a painful experience in this panic. I have lived through it in a very dreadful way. I cannot get over it—I cannot get the images of suffering out of my mind. It is a very real and a very awful thing to me—this wrecking of the lives of tens of thousands of people. And so I am hardly fitted for the amenities of social life just at present."

"But my father!" gasped she. "What has he to do with it?"

"Your father," he answered, "is one of the men who were responsible for that panic. He helped to make it; and he profited by it."

She started forward, clenching her hands and staring at him wildly. "Mr. Montague!" she exclaimed.

He did not reply.

There was a long pause. He could hear her breath coming quickly.

"Are you sure?" she whispered.

"Quite sure," said he.

Again there was silence.

"I do not know very much about my father's affairs," she began at last. "I cannot reply to what you say. It is very dreadful."

"Please understand me, Miss Hegan," said he. "I have no right to force such thoughts upon you; and perhaps I have made a mistake——"

"I should have preferred that you should tell me the truth," she said quickly.

"I believed that you would," he answered. "That was why I spoke."

"Was what he did so very dreadful?" asked the girl, in a low voice.

"I would prefer not to answer," said he. "I cannot judge your father. I am simply trying to protect myself. I'm afraid of the grip of this world upon me. I have followed the careers of so many men, one after another. They come into it, and it lays hold of them, and before they know it, they become corrupt. What I have seen here in the Metropolis has filled me with dismay, almost with terror. Every fibre of me cries out against it; and I mean to fight it—to fight it all my life. And so I do not care to make terms with it socially. When I have seen a man doing what I believe to be a dreadful wrong, I cannot go to his home, and shake his hand, and smile, and exchange the commonplaces of life with him."

It was a long time before Miss Hegan replied. Her voice was trembling.

"Mr. Montague," she said, "you must not think that I have not been troubled by these things. But what can one do? What is the remedy?"

"I do not know," he answered. "I wish that I did know. I can only tell you this, that I do not intend to rest until I have found out."

"What are you going to do?" she asked.

He replied: "I am going into politics. I am going to try to teach the people."